Pumpkin Spice and Mr. Right

L. Clara

To the girls who experienced bullying because of their
weight, you deserve all the love in the world.
To the animal lovers who would jump out of a moving car
to save an animal in need.
This is for you.

Content Warnings

Before continuing, please note this book contains:
Body image issues/body dysmorphia/fat shaming
Cheating by a previous partner/friend
Mention of loss of family members
Mention of death of animals (she's been a long-time vol-
unteer at kill shelters).
And eventually...sexually explicit scenes...I know a slow
burn from me? What is happening?
If any of these could be triggering, please proceed with
caution. Your mental health is more important to me than
you reading my book.

Contents

Prologue — 1

Chapter One — 7

Chapter Two — 13

Chapter Three — 18

Chapter Four — 24

Chapter Five — 30

Chapter Six — 35

Chapter Seven — 41

Chapter Eight — 46

Chapter Nine — 51

Chapter Ten — 56

Chapter Eleven — 61

Chapter Twelve — 65

Chapter Thirteen — 69

Chapter Fourteen 75

Chapter Fifteen 80

Chapter Sixteen 86

Chapter Seventeen 90

Chapter Eighteen 95

Chapter Nineteen 100

Chapter Twenty 104

Chapter Twenty-One 108

Chapter Twenty-Two 113

Chapter Twenty-Three 117

Chapter Twenty-Four 121

Chapter Twenty-Five 125

Chapter Twenty-Six 129

Chapter Twenty-Seven 134

Chapter Twenty-Eight 139

Chapter Twenty-Nine 143

Chapter Thirty 147

Chapter Thirty-One 152

Chapter Thirty-Two 156

Chapter Thirty-Three 161

Chapter Thirty-Four 166

Chapter Thirty-Five 171

Chapter Thirty-Six 174

Chapter Thirty-Seven   179

Chapter Thirty-Eight   183

Chapter Thirty-Nine   187

Chapter Forty   192

Chapter Forty-One   197

Chapter Forty-Two   201

Chapter Forty-Three   205

Epilogue   210

Afterword   215

Acknowledgements   217

About the Author   219

More by L. Clara   221

Fallon

Animals have been the light of my life for as far back as I can remember. Dogs, cats, rabbits, ferrets...if they're furry, chances are I would walk in front of oncoming traffic to rescue them. Although, I draw the line at reptiles and snakes. The creepy crawlies just aren't for me; I prefer fur. No one has ever really cared, let alone understood my love of animals, until I started volunteering at animal shelters. It's been one of the most rewarding experiences of my life. It's also one of the most heartbreaking.

For the last few years, I've been volunteering exclusively at shelters that euthanize the animals in their care. Is it fair? Absolutely, without a doubt, no, it is not. Is it something that unfortunately is a reality because of backyard breeders and puppy mills? Yes, and that's just to name a few of the reasons.

From the day I learned just how overpopulated the domestic pet population is, I wanted to do what I could to help. That's why I've volunteered at kill shelters for the last few years. These places also make sure that the animals are spayed or neutered before they are adopted so we can do our part to minimize irresponsible breeding. Don't get me started on the arguments I've had about that. I have one dog myself, the moment he was able to be sterilized I had it done to make sure we don't end up with even more animals in need down the road.

Marlow, he's my golden boy. My uncle bought him as a puppy—not something I like to talk about—and then he passed away not long after. I, of course, took Marlow in and he's been with me ever since. Marlow is the sweetest boy with the best hugs. He's the size of a moose, I swear. Golden retrievers are usually seventy-five pounds. But Marlow? My moose-man at his last weigh in was one hundred and twenty freaking pounds! He's a big boy.

He's been with me since he was only a few months old. He used to sleep on my head because it was closest to a window, the cool feeling of the glass against his fur kept him comfortable even on the hottest of nights. So freaking adorable.

It's been just over a week since the trajectory of my life changed and brought us here. Here being Hollow Heights, Illinois, a small town best known for its pumpkins. I'm quite impressed with how quickly I was able to pack up our life in my tiny apartment back in Arizona after the call. I loved the desert heat, but it's not every day you get an offer of your dream job. I mean how could I, Fallon Wilde, animal lover extraordinaire, turn down the opportunity to not only work to save animals, but get paid to do it? I may have loved everything about my home in Arizona, but when opportunity knocks, you've got to answer.

Besides, it's not like I have a man to discuss anything with anymore. My ex-fiancé left me for my best friend six months ago. Quite literally, nothing was keeping me in Arizona. As soon as the employment agreement was signed, I marched my happy ass down to the leasing office, gave them notice, and also gave my boss the heads up that I'd be leaving in a week.

May not be the norm for how far in advance either place wants to receive notice, but again, the animals need me.

Peace out corporate America, I'm off to rescue sweet little fur babies.

I may have thrown up the peace sign as I walked out of the office for the last time, but listen, Linda...They didn't even know my name unless I did something they didn't like. Not once in the ten years I worked there did anyone even so much as acknowledge my existence, unless it was a birthday. The executive assistant brought a cake for everyone to share, then they would say hi, only if I got in their way, of course.

My long black hair is a mess from the car karaoke that went down. I take out the hair tie and smooth down the wild mane before securing it back into place. A smile widens as I remember belting out songs from The Greatest Showman and Marlow howling along with me on the way here. Hugh Jackman and Zac Efron on the same soundtrack? How can you go wrong? Spoiler alert, you can't.

A crisp February breeze greets me as I step out of my old Hyundai Accent. It's packed full of everything I could fit in there and still had enough space for Marlow to stretch out in the back seat. It's not the first time I've had to wear a winter jacket, but I'm questioning my definition of a winter jacket as the chill finds its way deep into my bones.

My heart stutters in my chest at what's to come: excitement, anxiety, trepidation and so many more emotions course through my veins as I take in our new home. Cost of living here is much less than it was back in Arizona. Not only do I pay a little less, I also get a bit more space. Who could complain about that?

I close the door behind me after I exit the vehicle and take a step backward to open the door to get to Marlow. His fluffy tail is wagging back and forth so fast it's nearly invisible. I lean in to unhook his seatbelt. Yes, I have a doggie seatbelt. It's the safest way to travel. Have you not come to terms with the fact that I'm a crazy animal lady? Marlow's face is right in front of mine, licking off any remnants of makeup left on from the drive.

"Hi, my sweet fluffy little Macho Man." I coo into his fur as I unbuckle him.

The sweetest whimpers erupt from him as he jumps up, raising just his front paws to hug my neck as he tucks his head into my chest. My hands are in his fur petting and patting away. When he pulls away letting me know he's done with me, I stand tall and take a step back, letting him jump out. Marlow shakes and stretches out his cramped muscles. I feel the same way after being stuck in the car for three days straight, only stopping at the hotel long enough to sleep. I still have an hour until the landlord is here and I take this as the perfect opportunity to go explore the coffee shop a block away.

I really couldn't have found a better place to move into. The house is only three blocks from the shelter and one from, what is apparently, the best coffee shop to have ever existed. Do you want honesty? It was an online review on the coffee shop's year-round pumpkin coffee that sold me on accepting the position. Ok, not entirely, but it didn't hurt.

"Let's go see if they have any coffee left at The Caffeinated Pumpkin. Maybe they'll have some of those pup treats we read about!" I scratch behind Marlow's ears before connecting his leash and leading him in the direction the coffee shop is showing on my phone.

The walk only takes five minutes, which will save me on gas money. Money I'll no doubt spend on coffee if the coffee is as good as the reviews say. The intoxicating fragrance of freshly brewed beans gloriously floods my lungs. I haven't even walked in yet, and I can already tell if it tastes even half as good as it smells, I'm sold.

I tie up Marlow outside the door so I can still see him while I step inside to order. He lays down, waiting patiently for me to return. A pretty woman with light brown hair pulled back into a messy bun that rivals my own crazy hair stands behind the counter, a bright smile on her face. It's already noon but she's beaming like I'm the first person she's seen today.

"Hi! Welcome to The Caffeinated Pumpkin! I'm Elektra! And, yes, like the superhero. My dad was a fanboy, and my mom was still knocked out from the C-section when they handed over the birth certificate paperwork." She rushes out and giggles when she sees my eyes widen at how quickly she's speaking. "Sorry, I just had an extra shot. What can I get for you?"

A smile dances on my lips. I like her.

"Hi, Elektra, I'm Fallon, and my mom was a fan of Dynasty. The original, obviously." I snort out a laugh, "I'm new in town," *as in, 'I'm waiting for my new landlord to meet me with keys new in town,'* "and I heard the pumpkin coffee is to die for."

"I love that this was your first stop! We try to keep specialty flavors that are usually only available during the holidays elsewhere year-round, here." She grins, "I'll have that ready for you in a jiff! Do you need anything for that handsome boy you brought with you? I swear I can sense doggos a mile away. It's my superpower, I guess I had to get something from my name's sake."

"Yes, actually! He'd love a pup cake if you have any!" I respond excitedly.

"Sure!" Her response is equally enthusiastic as she walks away to make my drink. Elektra works quickly, returning with a large coffee in a to-go cup and a bag of six pup cakes. "On the house! Consider them a welcome to Hollow Heights!"

I stare at her in disbelief. I didn't think this kind of small-town welcome was still a thing. Guess I was wrong.

"Thank you so much! You're so kind." I feel a tightening in my chest, gratitude that someone who just met me could be so nice. The sweet gesture only reinforces the decision to move here, leaving those who hurt me back in Arizona.

I wave goodbye as I turn toward the door and exit back into the cool afternoon air. Marlow is sitting up, his tail wagging impatiently as he stares at the bag in my hands. My smart boy knows there is something special for him inside.

Chapter One

Four months later

My trusty companion is at my side, as usual, ready to face the day once we get our morning jolt and his peanut butter treat. He's already too heavy for his own good, so I had to cut back his daily pup cake habit within a few weeks of moving here. Really, what kind of dog mom would I be if I allowed him to get too big? The cool spring air has grown humid as the months move into summer. As strange as it sounds coming from someone who lived for the desert heat my entire life, I can't wait for my first full winter and season of sweater weather here. Plus, Elektra has been talking my ears off since I arrived in Hollow Heights about the incredible Addam's Farm Pumpkin Harvest that happens mid-October each year.

I take in the beautiful town that I've become a part of. The wide streets with beautiful lamp posts line the sidewalk on each side of the road. The main street in town was decorated beautifully for Valentine's Day when I first arrived in town, and I can't wait to see what they do for spooky season! A notification for an incoming email chirps on my phone just as I approach The Caffeinated Pumpkin.

> *From: Hollow Heights Animal Shelter*
>
> *To: Fallon Wilde*
>
> *Subject: Urgent at capacity*
>
> *Fallon,*
>
> *Urgent! We're at full capacity on the cat side of the shelter! We will need to find a way to get permanent placements or at least temporary foster placements outside of the shelter that can take them, or they will be euthanized.*
>
> *Thanks*
>
> *Tim*

The email from the night manager has me spiraling. It's not the first time this has happened, and unfortunately, it won't be the last. Yet, every single time, it breaks my heart into a million irreparable shards. It is, however, the first time I've had this happen first thing in the morning.

Hmm, I wonder if Carlisle and Esme would take in cats?

I force myself to laugh at my own joke. No, a fictional vampire family cannot help me right now. As I tie Marlow up to the post outside, I try to shake the anxious thoughts from my mind. I give my boy some scritches behind the ear and tell him to lay down, which he does.

I pull open the glass door, the incredible scent that is Elektra's Pumpkin Brew filling my nose and giving me hope that my day will get better. Before I can step inside, though, a mountain of a man walks in front of me. He rushes by everyone waiting to order until he gets to the opening in the counter. He obviously has his hands full, because he's putting a large box behind the counter before I can even register what it might have been. Why do the men in this town wear the tightest jeans? Jesus, you could bounce a quarter off that ass with how perfect it is. *Shit, why am I looking at his ass? He is an ass. I shouldn't be looking at it.* I raise my eyes to find a black T-shirt fitted so snugly across the barrel of his chest, it looks like his muscles will tear through it if he takes too deep of a breath. The more of him I take in, the more annoyed I am. He cut in front of me when I just needed some coffee to get through this already shitty morning. And just to add insult to injury, he has to look like *this*? Sandy colored hair peeks out from the damn cowboy hat he's wearing, his eyes just barely visible. But I can see the bright baby blues shining as he smiles warmly at anyone and everyone who meets his gaze.

"Good morning, kiddo!" He calls to Elektra, "How's the morning rush treating you?"

"Ugh, go away Ryker. I haven't had enough coffee for your morning sunshiny shit." She yawns as she pours a cup of coffee for the next customer in line.

"Good morning, Ryker," a few women in front of me purr at the man.

Gross. I silently groan to myself and force myself from rolling my eyes.

He tilts his cowboy hat at them politely as he continues to chat with Elektra. Once the rest of the line moves on with their drinks and breakfast pastries, he gives me a charming 'boy next door' smile. Elektra's face lights up when she sees me.

"Hey babe! Give me one sec, I've gotta grab Marlow's treat from the back. They just came out a few minutes ago so I left them back there to cool." She giggles and yells over her shoulder as she disappears into the kitchen space. "I'm vying for dog aunt of the year."

The cowboy's eyes are burning into me as Elektra and I chat. The moment I make the mistake of glancing in his direction, he takes the opening.

"Hi! You must be new in town; I haven't seen you here before. I'm Ryker..." He offers his hand, introducing himself.

"Hi," I reply curtly. "I've been here for a few months." Annoyed at the corny line, I try to shut the conversation down before it gets started. Does that shit really work on women? Granted, he is sexy as hell with a body obviously built for sin, but fuck that. Not interested, not after Kyle.

"Here ya go!" Elektra walks back in, carrying a small goodie bag for Marlow and oblivious to the tension between *Ryker* and me, based on the bright smile on her face. "It will be three dollars and seventy-five cents."

"My treat" Ryker says with his annoyingly handsome face, showing off a beautifully charming smile. I already hate him. I don't care that I don't know him.

"No, thank you. I can get my own drink." I respond as politely as possible, gritting my teeth so I don't say something rude.

"Please, allow me. A welcome to town gesture since I missed the original welcome wagon." He winks at me.

"Wait, there's a welcome wagon?" Elektra chimes in, confused by the direction the conversation has gone.

Ryker laughs, shaking his head. I smirk at her; she's adorable when she's clueless.

"If he's going to insist on paying for me, the least I can do is pay it forward." I hand over a five to my friend before turning to leave. "For the next customer," I smile at my friend. "I'll talk to you later."

"Come back on your way home, babe. I need to give my favorite fluffy guy some cuddles!" She calls after me as I rush out of my happy place.

The shelter is only two blocks away from Elektra's shop, so I untie my boy as we traipse through the thick, summer air. It's moments like this that I miss the desert. But only the climate. The people? Not so much.

The biggest perk of this job is getting to bring Marlow with me every day, tagging along for the behavioral assessments I give on the new rescues. It's helped him overcome his own anxieties about meeting new animals. Now he just wants to love everyone. Marlow sees a kiddie pool just inside the closed gate and pulls me to it. As soon as he gets his nose to the water, there's no point in even attempting to stop him. He flops in, splashing around and rolling a few times for good measure. I laugh, happily watching him enjoy his moment.

"Alright Macho Man, you've had your fun, let's go so we can find some of these sweet babies forever homes." I call to him. He glares at me and lets out an annoyed huff before shaking the water from his coat and following me into the air-conditioned building.

Walking through the main office, where we handle all our paperwork and adoptions, I'm reminded of the bullpen in The West Wing. We have four desks set up closely in the small room. It's not quite as large as The West Wing unfortunately, but it gives me the same vibes when we're down to the wire, hustling like our pants are on fire. We have less than eight hours to find homes for so many animals. And there will just be more tomorrow.

There are so many volunteers here already and it's not even eight in the morning. I just love how dedicated everyone is. I wave as I pass by Natalie and Megan who are in the cat room, changing out litter pans and loving on the felines that are currently here. My chest heaves as I take a deep breath, steadying my nerves. We have our work cut out for us today.

The next several hours are spent rushing around, making phone calls and sending messages to nearby rescues. The manager at Heavenly Paws, the godsend they are, informs me they can take five into foster care this afternoon. The Sebastian Foundation for Animal Rescue responds to my email, able to take one cat, at least it's something. But I still need at least four more transferred or in foster care by the end of the day. Our social media following is pretty active in following for updates and helping us find homes, so I decide to make a post with an urgent plea for local fosters.

Chapter Two

R ushing to the counter of Elektra's, or Elle as I call her, coffee shop, I secure the massive order behind her counter. I'm pretty sure I ran over one of her customers waiting in line, but I couldn't stop to check if I wanted these little orange guys to make it safely to their new home. Still wouldn't stop my momma from whooping my ass if she saw me being rude like this. I hear a tiny squeak from behind me as I carry the heavy ass box of pumpkins into The Caffeinated Pumpkin.

The place smells divine, as usual. Elle can do no wrong when it comes to baking, her grandma made sure of that. Her grandad was the one who taught her how to roast her own beans. She's perfected it over the few short years since she's taken over the place from her grandparents. But that's her story to tell.

"Hey, Kiddo!" I greet my favorite customer. Elle's family had a small piece of land down the road from our farm, and we would constantly find her in our patches growing up. She may be the little sister I never wanted, but growing up together made us as close as siblings. Really, it was fate that we would be friends.

"Ugh, go away Ryker, I haven't had enough coffee for your morning sunshiny shit." She yawns and pours a cup of coffee for the next customer. What no one in front of the counter sees is her stomping my toes in frustration at the *kiddo*. She hates any time I remind her I've got a couple of years on her.

As a few of the regulars say good morning, I notice Courtney and Lindsey smile widely at me like they do every time they see me. They never paid a lick of attention to me while we were in school, but now that they're grown and are ready to settle down, they both bother me every damn time I see them. I tip my hat at them and smile politely, just like my momma taught me, hoping the gesture gets me out of speaking to them.

When I turn my gaze back to Elle, she's got the widest grin on her face, one that rivals any she's given me, and she's been my best friend since our families met. "Hey, babe! Give me one sec, I've gotta grab Marlow's treat from the back. They just came out a few minutes ago so I left them back there to cool." She giggles and yells over her shoulder and she disappears into the kitchen space. "I'm vying for dog aunt of the year."

Before I can ask who Marlow is, I notice who she's talking to. Wow. Holy shit. Wow. I need more words in my vocabulary. This woman is stunning. I let my eyes rake over her body, taking in each gorgeous inch. She's in a pair of cut off shorts, showcasing the smooth, olive skin on her thick thighs. *Fuck, I'd love to get lost between those.* Based on the tight white tank top she's wearing, her stomach is soft, telling me she's not like the other women in town that live on salad alone. Speaking of soft, even beneath the simple tank, it's easy to see her tits are like pillows, soft and full. And they are calling. My. Name. Long black hair cascades down her shoulders like a curtain over her ample chest. When my gaze meets hers, her deep brown eyes are ready to cut through me if given the chance.

"Hi! You must be new in town; I haven't seen you here before. I'm Ryker…" I offer a hand over the counter.

"Hi. I've been here for a few months." Her response is short. Hrmm, she doesn't like me. Interesting.

"Here ya go!" Elle walks back in with an outstretched hand carrying a small bag and a bright smile still on her face, "it will be three dollars and seventy-five cents."

"My treat," I interject, pulling out my wallet from the back pocket of my jeans.

"No thank you, I can get my own drink." She is attempting to be polite, but I can see through the façade. She's irritated. I just don't know why.

"Please, allow me. A welcome to town gesture since I missed the original welcome wagon." I try a playful wink.

"Wait, there's a welcome wagon?" Elle chimes in, confused, and I inwardly groan at her naivety.

A moment later the woman is gone, striding out the door and into the summer sunshine. I don't miss the sway in her hips, or the way her thick, round ass fills out those shorts. Still, it bothers me that I don't know her name. Turning my attention back to my oldest friend, I find Elle glaring at me. "What?" I ask, confused.

"What did you do?" She asks accusingly, her hands planted firmly on her hips, just like her grandma. Mrs. Elias would scare the devil out of Hell if he came across her when she was fired up. "I haven't seen her like that the entire time she's lived here. Then you go and change your delivery time and suddenly she looks like someone just bought the last cup of pumpkin coffee before she could get her fix."

I snort which makes her eyes go wide, nearly bugging out of her head.

"Oh my god! What did you do?" She basically screams the question at me, drawing the stares of the few customers still inside.

"Calm down, Elle!" I laugh at her ridiculousness. "All I did was say 'hello.' I don't know why she acted so put off. I didn't do anything different than I usually do when I come by." I shrug my shoulders, still unclear how I offended the beautiful woman who's name I still didn't know.

"I swear Ryker...she's become a good friend the past few months since she's been here and she's running the shelter. Don't be a dick!" Elle growls at me. It's kind of cute that this tiny little thing thinks she scares me. I tower over her five-foot two frame, standing at six feet, even without my work boots.

"I didn't do anything other than say hello and try to introduce myself." I decide to press my luck and prod my friend for more information. "What's her name? She didn't tell me." She glares at me then rolls her eyes.

"Her name is Fallon. She moved here four months ago from Arizona. Her dog is the golden retriever that was tied up outside. She takes him everywhere."

"The job at the shelter is what brought her here?" I question, surprised that she would pick up and move for a job like that.

"The job at the shelter, among other things, but you know how you say I'm the animal whisperer?" She arches a brow as a smile dances on her lips.

"Of course! You're the reason that Mr. Feeny sleeps under my damn porch and comes running for me every evening when I come back to the house!" I smile when I think about the fox that has claimed me as his own.

Fox distribution system is as much a thing as the cat distribution system, at least when Elle comes around.

"Don't even act like you don't do the Feeny call whenever you think you're alone." Elle teases, her voice full of humor.

I can't even deny it. I do the call, every night, without fail.

"Anyway, what about you being the animal whisperer?" I ask, trying to get us back on topic.

"That woman has run into oncoming traffic to save a dog that was hit by a car." I gape at the surprising tidbit of information. Elle smirks at me. "I've got nothing on her."

"I get it, the title has been passed on to her." I pause, looking down at my feet as I try to think of a way to ask Elle what I *really* want to know. "So," I ask as nonchalantly as possible. "Does she come by every day around this time?"

Chapter Three

Whalon

W hen I check the time, I'm surprised to see it's already two in the afternoon. My stomach growls, reminding me that I haven't had lunch yet. Groaning, I sneak a pack of peanut butter crackers from my desk drawer, opening them as quietly as possible. If Marlow hears the wrapper, he'll be up in two seconds flat, begging for his share. I glance over to find him still snoozing away, so I start nibbling on my snack, reminding myself I need to be better about bringing real food in to eat. Quickly scarfing them down and disposing of the evidence, I gently pet Marlow's head, waking him.

"Hey bud, you wanna go for a walk?"

He flops his head back down with an annoyed grunt. I chuckle to myself before grabbing my wallet from my desk. Heading out, I make sure to lock up my office so Marlow can't get out, then I head to Elektra's for my afternoon dose of coffee. Some may say it's a problem. They would be wrong.

The short walk from the shelter to the coffee shop feels refreshing in its own way. Sometimes stepping away from the chaos of the shelter is exactly what I need to reset my mind. Elektra sees me through the door as I approach, waving with a bright smile on her face as always. I pull the glass door open and step inside, an overwhelming blast of cold air hitting me as soon as I enter. The drastic difference between the outside and in is almost too much. Before I can even ask, I'm handed a fresh cup of pumpkin spice coffee. I grin at my friend as I take a sip.

"Mmm, thank you," I breathe, the hot liquid warming my chilled body from the inside out.

"You're welcome, Bestie Boo. Now, where is my nephew?" She looks over my shoulder to where Marlow usually waits outside.

I snort at her nickname for me. "He decided sleep was more important. It's been a rough morning," I explain, reminded of Marlow, snoozing away in my office.

"What happened? What did Ryker do? I knew he did something stupid." The words fly out of Elektra's mouth as fire fills her eyes.

My eyes find hers and I try to mask my expression before I speak.

"Who?" I ask, feigning ignorance. Maybe if I act like I don't remember him, I can pretend his annoyingly gorgeous ass hasn't been running through my mind all day.

"My friend that was here earlier?" She questions, "So, wait, he didn't piss you off?"

"The cowboy? No." An amused snort escapes before I can explain. "I got an email from Tim just before I got here. We were at capacity for the cat rooms. I've been making calls all day for spots at nearby rescue groups and fosters. I just had enough time to step out to grab this and grab something a little more satisfying than the crackers I have at work."

"Ah! I have just the thing for you!" She squeals before squatting down behind the counter to pull out a pumpkin croissant with a cinnamon brown sugar drizzle over the top. "Nuke it for 15 seconds when you get back to the shelter and you'll love me forever." She grins as she hands me the pastry in a beautiful orange box with The Caffeinated Pumpkin's logo on top.

"I already do," I tease her. I reach to pull out my wallet, but Elektra shakes her head at me. "Not today, lady. Just bring my boy by the shop on your way home." She smiles and shoos me away.

"See you later, thank you again!" With a smile and wave, I exit the shop.

I sit here with the last bite of the croissant, amazed at how talented my best friend is. It's the most freaking delicious thing I've ever put in my mouth. My desk phone rings loudly,startling me out of my thoughts. I pick it up and bring the receiver to my ear.

"Hollow Heights Animal Shelter, this is Fallon. How may I help you?"

"Hey! It's Shelby, do you still need any fosters? I have space for either two adults or a momma and babies." One of my most enthusiastic volunteers and foster mom's voice greets me on the other line.

"Oh, my goodness, Shelby, you're an angel! How do you feel about bottle feeders? We have a litter of four that just came in an hour ago." I cross my fingers hoping she's able to help. I can see the momma and her babies in my head, their cute little black and white heads nuzzled together in their cage. I really don't want to keep them here any longer than necessary.

"Ugh! I can't say no to that. Ok. I'll take the bottle feeders and their momma. Bentley is ready for a new 'project kitty.'" She laughs into the phone. Her resident grumpy cat always perks up when they have a new feline in the home. Once he feels the foster is ready to be rehomed, he completely ignores that cat. I don't question it; Bentley hasn't been wrong, and all of those cats have found amazing furever homes.

"Have I mentioned lately just how fantastic you are?" I grin as I make a note and send a message back to the person in the cat room, letting them know Shelby will be by to pick up our furry friends soon.

"Yea, yea." She giggles, "I'll see you in twenty."

We hang up and I go back to my social media messages to find six requests to foster cats, four for dogs, and a handful of people requesting adoption for some of the longer-term residents on both sides. My heart swells with so much pride and joy. I did it! Well, at least for today.

All the fosters and rescues have picked up their animals by five p.m.. The paperwork is completed and filed by five fifteen and my last task before I finish my day is a thank you post on our social media accounts.

> *Huge thank you to everyone who shared and engaged with our posts throughout the day. We were able to make enough space for the night so that no lives were lost today. This community is incredible, and you are all appreciated so very much.*
>
> *Until tomorrow,*
>
> *Fallon and the family of staff and volunteers of Hollow Heights Animal Shelter*

I smile to myself for a job well done before I shut off my computer for the night. My gaze turns to where Marlow is laying on his back, his limbs sprawled in all directions. Chuckling to myself, I stand and stretch out the kinks in my own muscles from sitting for so long. Maybe I need to keep a yoga mat in here so I can stretch a bit during the day on marathon work days like today.

"Macho Man, it's time to go!" I call to him. He rolls over and jumps to his feet, shaking out the sleep. He darts to the closed office door, his tail wagging so fast it's a blur. I grab his leash and secure it before we head out into the summer heat.

As we approach our usual stop, I notice Elektra waiting for us out front, just a second before Marlow spots her based on the pull on the leash. I drop the leash knowing it's going to be easier and safer for everyone involved if he gets access to his favorite person– besides me– sooner rather than later. I hear a shrill squeal and see my friend tumble onto her butt. She's giggling up a storm as I approach, all while Marlow licks her face like he hasn't seen her in a year and not just hours ago. This is our daily routine; I take him to work, and the three of us walk home together.

One thing Elektra forgot to mention when we met all those months ago is that she's my landlord. She refurbished the two-story house and made it into two spacious apartments. It's cozy as hell and we get to hang out all the time. I really won in all aspects of this entire relocation situation.

Marlow finally allows my bestie to stand, and she takes his leash to lead him the rest of the way home. We walk in a comfortable silence, the evening air slightly less overwhelming than the heat and humidity earlier today. It's only a few minutes before we're back at our place and she releases Marlow from the leash so he can run around the yard.

"What do you think about fried chicken and mac and cheese for dinner?" She asks as she unlocks the front door.

"Sure. You make the chicken; I'll make the mac and cheese?" I ask, stepping inside the cool house. Thank Christ for air conditioning.

She arches a brow at me with an unspoken question.

"Yes, I'll put the crackers on top, you weirdo," I laugh and call Marlow inside behind us so we can cook in our own places before we share a meal together on the back patio. This has become our normal end of day routine since I moved in upstairs. One of us makes the main course, the other makes a side. The first time I made mac and cheese, my mom's recipe, Elektra lost her damn mind because of the crispy cracker crumbs on top. The second time, I ran out of crackers, and she looked at me like I was the devil. Obviously, she hasn't let me live it down.

"Love you!" she calls to me as she walks through her door where Marlow follows. Rude.

Chapter Four

I t's five-thirty by the time I finally get to sit down after working in my family's pumpkin fields since the crack of dawn. While my mind usually tends to reflect on the day's events and how I can improve the process for the next day, all I can focus on right now is how glad I am that my assistant, Jake, couldn't make it in this morning. I haven't been able to stop thinking about the woman from Elle's all day. I pick up the beer I had grabbed from my fridge before returning to the porch. My mouth wraps around the lip of the bottle and I take in a long pull. The fizzy feeling tickles my nose as I drink.

"Mr. Feeny!" I call out and chuckle before I do exactly what Elle accused me of earlier "Mr. Fee he he he heeeeneeyyyy!" I bellow.

I can't get my voice as high as Eric Matthews, but my little red fox comes out of hiding all the same.

"Hey, friend," I pat his furry head and scritch behind his ears as he sits by my feet, just enjoying one another's company. "Can I send Elle a picture?" I ask, like he understands what I'm saying. Although, I'm pretty sure he does, when he sits up and opens his little mouth like he's smiling. I pull out my phone so I can snap a quick picture and send it off to Elle.

Ryker:

Asked him to send you a picture and he posed.

Elle:

It's because he loves me most.

Ryker:

Obviously. I'm certain if you let him follow you home, he'd move in with you.

Elle:

I don't think any of us would mind that actually.

Ryker:

Any? What are you talking about?

Elle:

I swear you pay no attention to me. I've told you how many times now I have a new tenant.

Ryker:

I know that, but why would your tenant have anything to say about you getting a pet?

A picture is included with the last message. Fallon and Marlow are sitting on the back patio that Elle and I have eaten on many times before. She looks even more beautiful than she did earlier this morning. She's wearing a pair of yoga pants that are like a second skin and a thin T-shirt that hugs her curves perfectly. Have I really been that busy the last few months? She's been over here once a week for dinner like usual, but I haven't gone to her place in a while. I just figured Elle was coming over to see Feeny.

I laugh at the response. She's not wrong on that, not in the least. I smirk to myself the entire time I'm finishing my drink. Tomorrow is going to be a fun day.

The sun has barely peeked over the horizon and I'm already in the fields checking the patches. It takes a few hours for Jake and I to check all the pumpkins, ensuring none were destroyed overnight by critters or frost. The greenhouse plants were just started not long ago so we can check on those later this afternoon. We try to stay in the patches the furthest out for our business and personal pickings. The ones closer to town are the ones that we open during the pumpkin fest for visitors to use. We load up another half a dozen gourds to take into The Caffeinated Pumpkin along with a few other local business and personal deliveries. It's seven-thirty by the time we finish up long enough for a break. This is usually when Jake will do some local deliveries. Today, I've decided to take one stop off his route—Elle's shop.

I grin when I pull up and see her just turning the sign to show that the shop is open. Grabbing the box of gourds, I make my way inside, juggling my delivery box as I open the door. "Hi, friend," I say to her as soon as I walk in. My voice is chipper, as it always is at this time of day. It's not *my* fault she's a night owl and hates to be up before the sun.

"Oh god, why are *you* here and so early on top of that?" She asks as she starts the coffee machines. The full pastry cases are already prepped and ready for the morning rush.

"What? A man can't decide to personally deliver your order from now on?" I ask with my most charming smile .

She levels me with a glare, her hands going to her hips, "Did you fire Jake?"

"Of course not. He's just got other deliveries. I wanted to take you off his plate since I know how absolutely delightful you can be before you have coffee in the morning." A laugh bursts free from my chest as I give her a hard time.

"Ok. How many did you bring me this time?" She asks as she looks in the box with a brow raised.

Before she can call me out on my bullshit, the door swings open.

"Coffee. Stat." Fallon's voice fills the otherwise quiet space. "Must. Have. Coffee," she walks in looking as exhausted as Elle.

"Well, hello again. It's nice to see you this morning, beautiful." A smirk dances on my lips as I take in her luscious form. She's dressed in another pair of jean shorts but today she's wearing a graphic T-shirt with an image of a sloth hanging from one of those "slow" signs construction workers hold up and the words *Don't Speed* at the bottom. The neck has been cut to give it a generous V shape, showing off the tops of her breasts.

"Oh. Hi," She stutters, glancing between Elle and me questioningly. "Sorry, did I interrupt something?

"Ew! Bestie Boo, that's gross. He's like my brother." Elle dramatically gags before making formal introductions, "Ryker, Fallon, Fallon, Ryker."

"It's nice to officially meet you, Fallon. Welcome to Hollow Heights." She stares at my outstretched hand like it's a bomb that might detonate at any second. "I didn't realize you were living at Elle's rental unit."

"It's nice to meet you too," She hesitates, "I'm running late, can I grab the coffee, and I'll swing by this afternoon?" Fallon shuffles her feet nervously, glancing at her watch.

"Fine, but make sure you eat today!" Elle points a stern finger at the girl that's been occupying all of my thoughts since yesterday.

Fallon pulls out her wallet to pay, but I shake my head, "My treat."

She digs around for cash, fishing out a few dollar bills, "no, you did that yesterday" She rolls her eyes as I slap a five on the counter.

"And I will continue to do so every morning that I'm here when you are," I wink at her with a mischievous smile.

She doesn't bother arguing with me this time. I expected backlash, but maybe she really is running late. I shrug, not much else I can do about it since she all but ran out as soon as Elle handed over the drink, throwing a quick '*bye*' over her shoulder before disappearing out of sight.

Elle clears her throat, bringing my attention back to her and the box as she nods to the contents, "You and I both know this will barely last me until tomorrow."

"No? Guess that means I'll have to come back tomorrow. What a shame…" I grin at her before sauntering back out to my truck.

Chapter Five

Fallon

Today's tasks have been centered around planning an adoption event. I know this town is small, but these types of things can bring people from different areas, increasing our chances of finding homes for our animals. We need to utilize our social media following to bring more people out to take part, even if it's just donations to help with the animals we do have or to possibly expand the size of the shelter. If we could build an addition, we could not only save more animals, but employ more people. Really, it's a win, win.

I start the day by reaching out to the local pet store to see if we can advertise there. We need to evaluate the interest before anything can be planned on a larger scale. The phone has been ringing in my ear for a few moments before someone finally answers.

"Woof 'n Tails, this is Fannie." A nasally voice says as soon as she answers the call.

"Hi Fannie! This is Fallon from Hollow Heights Animal Shelter." I somehow got lucky, and the owner is the one on the other line, remembering her name from when I checked out the store's website last night. "I wanted to see if we could discuss something that could potentially benefit us both."

"Oh, you're the new girl that's just started up there. I've heard about you." She responds with a lighthearted laugh.

"Yes ma'am," I chuckle.

"Well, what can I do for ya here, sweetheart?" She leaves no time for beating around the bush. I can appreciate that.

"I wanted to try an adoption event outside of the shelter walls. Yes, they can be fine in a pinch, but when I was in Arizona if we held any events outside the shelter our number of adoptions increased significantly." There's a pregnant pause and when she doesn't respond I go on, "if we have it at your pet shop it could lead to more sales for you that day, as well. People adopting new pets will need bags of food, crates, leashes..." I list off a few of the animal essentials, hoping to entice her with a possible increase to her bottom line.

"Ok, ok. I get it," I can hear the smile in her voice. "When do you want to do this?" She asks.

"How about a week from Saturday?" I grin at her response.

"Get me a flyer to review by the end of the day and we're in," She sounds as excited as I am.

"I can be there in an hour with a mockup."

"You don't have to bring it down," she laughs.

"I don't mind, plus, Marlow needs a new bag of food." My heart skips a beat with excitement. I pull out my personal laptop so I can use the photo editing software. What can I say, I take my promotional material seriously. The next thirty minutes are spent meticulously creating a flyer that will not only be eye catching for potential adopters but also donors. Once I'm satisfied with the image placement and confident that the information is correct, I press print. Marlow is snoozing, so instead of waking him for a walk, I kneel down and press a quick kiss to his head. Sneaking out of the office, I quietly close the door and slip outside.

My walk to Woof 'n Tails is quick, since they're only a few blocks away. Yet another reason why I love this small town. I can walk just about anywhere in under ten minutes. As soon as I enter the shop I'm greeted by an older woman, her silver hair spiked and styled in a short pixie cut. The Woof 'n Tails T-shirt hangs loose on her small frame; a pair of snug light-colored jeans hugging her slender thighs are a contrast to the oversized shirt.

"Good afternoon, welcome to Woof 'n Tails!" She beams at me, "I'm Fannie, let me know if I can help you with anything."

"Ahh, just the person I was looking for!" I grin at her, "I'm Fallon, from the shelter. It's so nice to meet you."

"Damn girl, you work fast." She chuckles, "It's nice to meet you too."

I laugh in response, "I try to be efficient. I'm really stoked to see how this event works for both of us. I know it's still in town and not far from the shelter, but I think the off-site could be so beneficial as I mentioned earlier." I hand over the flyer and her eyes widen.

"You just made this since we spoke?" Fannie's eyes dart back to me, "this is amazing."

"Thank you," I smile shyly at her, not used to the praise.

"Let's get this out there. Can I post this up front awhile?" There is so much joy in her eyes.

I nod my head, "Yes, of course! I'll head back and have more copies printed to post around town. We will get a post up on our social media and start getting volunteers signed up to come help out." Before I can stop myself, I lunge forward and wrap my arms around her shoulders, "Thank you so much."

"You are very welcome sweetheart, animals have been my passion since I was a kid, I understand where your heart is." She responds as she pats my back reassuringly.

Overcome with excitement and so many things added to my to-do list, I nearly forget the other reason I wanted to come here in person. I find a fifteen-pound bag of the brand of food Marlow likes and carry it up to the cash register. After a few more minutes of conversation with Fannie, I tell her I'll keep in touch with any updates and expectations and ask her to do the same for me.

The walk back is a bit slower and I'm second guessing my life choices carrying this bag back to the shelter. I'm half-tempted to make a right to drop it off at the coffee shop but before I can, I hear my name from across the street.

"Fallon?" The voice is familiar. I turn my head to see Ryker in a truck stopped in the actual middle of the street. The vehicle is facing in the opposite direction of where I'm going.

Will this man just leave me alone?

"Hi, Ryker," I half-heartedly wave to him and decide to continue to the shelter, not wanting to make small talk.

"Let me give you a ride so you don't have to carry that bag." He sounds so sincere and sweet. It only irritates me further. And he's still just sitting in the middle of the street.

"No, it's ok. I've got it," I respond while I continue to walk. I don't bother looking back, just keeping my eyes on the road toward my destination. Before I realize what's happening, the bag has been removed from my arms. "What the –"

"If you don't want to get in my truck, I'll just walk with you." The smile is both charming and genuine. And it irritates my soul. Did he seriously leave his truck in the middle of the road to walk over here? Oh, he must have parked on the side of the road before he absconded with my dog food. This man.

"Ryker, it's fine. I'm a big girl, I can take care of things myself., I roll my eyes at his unwanted show of chivalry.

"I'm sure you can take care of yourself, beautiful, but let me help this time?" The smirk dancing on his lips has butterflies doing a number on my stomach. "Besides, if my momma finds out I let you carry this bag all the way back to wherever it is you're going, she will tan my hide, even if I am a grown man."

"Don't worry, I won't tell your mom, just let me –" I try to argue but he continues walking in the direction I was headed. "Ryker!" I chase after him, the tight jeans making his ass look good enough to bite, while the cowboy hat he's wearing is, yet again, doing something to my insides that I'm not happy about.

"Yes, Darlin'?" I can hear the smile in his voice. "So, where are we going?"

"*I'm* going back to the shelter." I say pointedly. "Don't you have something better to do?" I groan as I motion to continue walking straight.

"I don't think there is anything better I could be doing with my time right now," He looks over at me and winks.

Hells bells.

Chapter Six

Never in my life have I been so happy to have had to run into town to grab a part for my tractor. As soon as I had attempted to start it this afternoon, the engine wouldn't turn over. Luckily for me, it's just a blown fuse. What's even more lucky for me, though? The fact that I am driving my truck down Hollow Road to find Fallon lugging a big ass bag of dog food.

Stubborn woman tried to fight me on helping her get to where she's going too, but it only took a few minutes to break her down and agree to let me help. Granted, I hadn't given her much of a choice, refusing to let her ignore me when I called her from the cab of my truck, but it's fine. All that matters is that I convinced her. And apparently I have zero problem with hastily parking my truck on the side of the road for this woman.

We walk in silence for a few moments before I open my mouth. "So, tell me about yourself, Darlin'," Glancing down, I find her eyeing me.

"What do you want to know?" She groans.

"Everything," the answer comes out easily. For the first time in years, I do want to know everything about someone, the beautiful woman next to me in particular.

"I moved here earlier this year. I love my job. Animals are better than most people." She shrugs. "That about sums me up."

"I think I already knew all of that," I tease. "Tell me something no one knows."

"Why?"

"Why not?" I test her with a mischievous smirk, "Are you hiding something?"

She pauses mid-step and turns to me. An expression I can't decipher briefly graces her face, disappearing just as quickly before she speaks again.

"My life back in Arizona is in my past. I'm not hiding anything; I just don't want to talk about it." She lets out a deep breath, "May I ask you something?"

"Anything, darlin'." I reply as we approach the shelter.

"Why are you so determined to get to know me?" She stops dead in her tracks and levels me with a "don't bullshit me" look.

"There's something unique about you, something that keeps drawing me to you, like a magnet. I can't shake it. I can't shake *you*." I shrug, having no problem answering her question honestly.

"I don't get it." Fallon groans, her hands firmly on her hips as her eyes flash with emotion. "There isn't anything special about me, Ry." She turns, continuing into the shelter without allowing me to respond.

I'm stunned silent for a brief moment as my brain tries to play catch up to whatever the fuck that was. Snapping back to the present, I chase after her. She approaches a closed door and I'm there as soon as she turns the knob. Stepping inside with her, I drop the bag of dog food onto the chair sitting in front of what has to be her desk.

My heart hammers in my chest as I turn to see her waiting by the open door for me to take my leave. I feel a low growl deep in my chest as I cross the distance to her. She yelps when my hands land on either side of her head, caging her. I'm so close I can almost feel the hitch in her breath. Her chest heaves, rising and falling in a quick rhythm. But is her rapid breathing from excitement? Or fear? I lift her chin to meet my gaze, smirking when I find her eyes half lidded with lust.

"You don't see yourself clearly, Darlin', don't worry I'll change that." I grin at her, keeping my eyes on hers for several beats. My cock strains against my jeans and I take a few steadying breaths before I hear a warning growl. I cautiously step away from Fallon to see a beautiful golden retriever with his teeth bared.

"It's alright bud, I'm fine." Fallon pants out, patting her leg for him to come to her. He does as he's told.

"Good boy, taking care of your momma." I wink at her. "Don't worry, I won't do anything she doesn't like."

I kneel down and hold a hand out for the dog to come to me. He glances up to Fallon who has started coughing at my comment before he walks over. I pat his head and fluff up the fur around his neck.

"Such a good boy, aren't you?" I coo at the dog. "I'm going to take the food with me and drop it off at Elle's since I have a key." I glance up to find a very shy and speechless Fallon, "I'll see you tomorrow, Darlin'."

I don't let her respond before I lift the bag easily from the chair, tossing it over my shoulder as I leave the shelter. It's a fifteen-minute walk back to where I left my truck on the side of the road, but it gives me time to run through our interaction in Fallon's office. The bed of my truck is empty of pumpkins or equipment for the first time in a while, so I toss the bag in before sliding into the front seat. I grab my phone from my pocket and pull up my text thread with Elle.

Ryker:

I'm dropping off a bag of dog food in your apartment in case you get there before Fallon.

Elle:

Why?

Ryker:

Because you and I both know if Momma found out I let Fallon carry it all the way from Woof 'n Tails to the shelter then back to your place, she would beat my ass. Even if I'm almost thirty-five and running the farm on my own.

Elle:

Wait, why were you at the pet shop? Oh! Are you finally getting a pet? What are you getting? Can I name it?

Ryker:

God, you're a pain. I had to come into town for a damn fuse for the tractor. I saw her walking from the pet shop toward the shelter with a big ass bag of dog food. I offered to drive her, but she refused, so I walked her back to the shelter. But again, if momma knew I let her carry it home…

Elle:

Aw! Momma Addams will be so proud when we see her next week!

Ryker:

I can't stand you.

Elle:

Liar.

My drive to Elle's is quick. It's both convenient and annoying as hell how close she is to everything in town. She barely has space to breathe. But it's her space and she loves it. I prefer everything about my farm, the space, the animals. I park my truck out front and make quick work of getting the bag of food inside, but once I'm in Elle's place I can't help but pause, noticing a pen and notepad on the coffee table. Grabbing each, my heart thuds rapidly as I write a quick note. Fuck it, I've got to shoot my shot.

Fallon,

I enjoyed our walk. Looking forward to getting to know you as the days go on. Don't hesitate to give me a call if you ever need anything.

Ryker

I finish it off with my number and leave the note on top of the dog food and head out before I change my mind.

I'll see her soon.

Chapter Seven

I've never been so turned on in my entire life. And by this moth-erfucker, of all people! I've been so clear! *Haven't I been clear?* No matter how many times I'm cold and show no interest, he just continues to push. I groan, tilting my head back against the wall where he left me fucking panting for him. *Fucking Ryker.*

Marlow presses his nose into my hand to pull me out of my frozen stupor. I physically shake my head trying to rid my thoughts of the man that refuses to leave me alone. My hands glide through my Macho Man's silky golden fur.

"I'm ok, buddy." I blow out a deep breath. "How about we try to get some posts done and call it a day? I can work on everything else from home." I pad over to my desk on shaky legs and unlock the shelter computer.

I send an email blast out about the upcoming event to get fosters for the dogs we have. We can only take a handful of cats due to the excessive heat outside and there is only so much space where we can keep them inside the store. Once the message is sent to the fosters, I reach out to our volunteers. I create a handful of posts to go up at scheduled times across all of our social media platforms to announce it by the end of the workday.

By the time that is done, I've already received a handful of responses from both fosters and volunteers. Everyone is as excited as Fannie and I are at the possibilities that this could bring for the shelter and the animals we help. There are so many lives that will be saved if this goes as well as I'm hoping.

It's four p.m. by the time I lift my eyes from the computer screen. My stomach growls and I realize I forgot to eat. Again. Crap. I really need to start packing a lunch. I quickly shut down the computer and grab my personal laptop, stuffing it into my bag.

"Hey, bud, let's get going." I call Marlow, who stands up and shakes out the sleep and laziness he's enjoyed today. He picks up his leash from next to the dog bed in his mouth and brings it over to me, dropping it into my open palm. "Good boy!" I praise him and clip the leash onto his collar.

We walk at a leisurely pace back to the house. I text Elektra when we're on our way to let her know I'm leaving early, and I'll see her at home. She responds quickly,

Elektra:

You forgot to eat again, didn't you?

Damn her for knowing me so well.

Fallon:

That's not the reason I'm leaving early!

Elektra:

That doesn't answer my question, bestie boo!

Fallon:

I'm not going to answer your question.

Elektra:

Don't wait for me to eat, stubborn ass. I won't be home till later.

Fallon:

Oo! Hot date?

Elektra:

Ew, I'm having dinner at the Addams' Farm. Oh! Speaking of, Ryker left Marlow's food inside my apartment. There is a spare key to my place taped to the top of the bottom shelf of your bookcase.

Fallon:

How is that speaking of? And why? You know what, I don't need to know. Thank you, have fun!

My walk home is easy and relaxing, luckily it doesn't take too long. I'm thankful for technology because only five minutes after I get Marlow settled inside, the pizza I had ordered on my walk arrives. I carry the box up to my kitchen and grab a plate. My mind goes to the food I bought for Marlow and before I sit down to eat my own dinner, I find the key that Elektra hid in my apartment and go downstairs to her door. The key slides into the lock easily enough and the telltale sound of the lock disengaging lets me know it unlocked just as easily.

It's just inside, by her table, exactly where he said he'd put it. I see a note on top of the bag, but I just shove it into my pocket before I lift the bag into my arms and carry it up the steps to my apartment. Okay, I may be glad that he made me give him the bag. This thing is awkward AF to carry. Marlow is sitting at the top of the stairs, his tail wagging to the point of near invisibility again. The fact he knows what this bag is cracks me up.

"Ok, bud, sit. I'll get you some now." I say to the hyper dog before I tear open the bag and pour some into his bowl.

Once he's settled and eating his dinner, I carry my own plate into the living room with an ice-cold bottle of Modelo. I curl up on the couch and pick up the latest book by K.D. Smalls. What can I say? I'm ready for spooky season and a paranormal romance is a good place to start. No, let's be real, it's more about the why choose aspect of it. I don't see myself dating one, let alone three men, but damn, Everly has it made with all that cock.

I lift the bottle to my lips and take a long pull of the drink. The sweet flavors of the beer burst on my taste buds as the fizzy feeling tickles my nose. I shift in my seat to put the bottle back down and hear a crinkle of paper. Realization hits me that I put the note from Elektra's in my back pocket. I dig out the paper and unfold it, scanning over the words.

A smirk twists at my lips. I really don't get why he's trying so hard. Shit, Kyle didn't even try this hard, and we were engaged for Christ's sake. I'm not sure if it's the buzz of the little bit of alcohol or the story I've been reading, but I'm feeling a tad less stabby than I usually am. Picking up my phone from the arm of the couch, I open my text messages. I roll my eyes as I enter his number and type up a short text. Concise. Straight to the point.

Fallon:

Thank you.

Chapter Eight

It's been a week since Fallon's introduction threw my entire world into an upheaval. Don't get me wrong, I've loved every second of it; she's a firecracker and I can't get enough of her sass and attitude. She's got brick walls built higher than the Eiffel Tower but I think I'm slowly breaking through them. It helps that Marlow likes me at least. I've made it a point when I see her for her morning coffee to walk outside after her so I can give Marlow one of Elle's treats.

I pulled up a few minutes earlier than usual this morning, so Elle put me to work unloading the pumpkins into the kitchen. Honestly, I think she's enjoying how long it's taking me to ask Fallon on a date. I have the last gourd in my hand when I hear Elle's voice.

"Good morning, Bestie Boo!" She's already down half a cup of coffee so her chipper tone is mostly genuine right now.

I hear Fallon say something, but I can't quite make it out. Not wanting to waste any more time, I step out of the kitchen and am greeted by a smirk. Ahh ha! She is warming up to me!

"Good morning, Darlin'," I say as soon as she sees me.

"Morning, Ryker," She tries to sound annoyed, but I can hear the light amusement hiding beneath it.

My brow furrows when I see the top she chose for today. A white T-shirt, the neck custom cut again, this one has a purple squirrel with the fluffiest of tails, it could give Mr. Feeny a complex. It has the words "K.D. Smalls: Nuts, Spice and Everything Not So Nice."

"I have questions. So many questions, beautiful." I chuckle, my eyes landing on hers. My heart thumps harder when I see her smiling back at me.

Fallon's phone chips in her pocket and when she pulls out the device to check the notification she tenses.

"Welp, you know where to find me. For now, I have some last-minute things to do for the event. It's only two days away!" Fallon sounds overwhelmed.

"What do you need help with?" I step around the counter, ready to ignore my responsibilities for the day to make sure she's not overworking herself.

She shakes her head as she responds, "I'll be fine! I've got no time to chat today, though. See you both later!"

In the blink of an eye, she's out the door with her coffee in one hand and Marlow's leash in the other. They both disappear out of sight quickly and I'm left feeling disappointed at her absence. I turn toward Elle who just shrugs in response.

"She won't ask for help, Ryker, and she'll fight you every step of the way if you try." Elle's eyes lock on mine. "Fallon's stubborn, not unlike someone else I know." She pins me with a knowing look.

"I'll be fine," I smirk back at her as I head toward the door.

"Famous last words, dumbass. Make sure she eats!" She yells after me.

After I left Elle, I had to run back to the farm to make sure all the two person tasks were completed for the day before I left Jake on his own. If I didn't love the asshat like a brother, I would have sucker punched him for the catcall I got when I explained where I was headed. I pull up to the shelter after making a pit stop at Marco's pizza, a medium chicken parm pie boxed up and sitting in the seat next to me. When Elle told me yesterday that Fallon has forgotten to eat lunch for the past two weeks, I was pissed. She should be taking better care of herself.

I step out of my truck with pizza in hand and a pup cake balancing on top of the box. Obviously, I can't come empty handed when Marlow is the way to her heart. A young woman is exiting the shelter with a cat carrier and a huge grin on their face. She holds the door for me until I get there and waves in greeting.

"Congratulations, ma'am." I smile and tip my hat at her. She blushes, scurrying away as I step through the doorway.

I make my way through the shelter, taking the same path as when I followed Fallon last week. The door is open, so I walk straight in as if she's expecting me, only there's no Fallon to be seen. I slide a few papers out of the way before I place the pizza down on the desk and pull my phone from my pocket to shoot off a quick text. I know she doesn't take Marlow on midday walks so she can't be far.

Hey Darlin', what are you doing?

Finalizing an adoption. Why?

I don't bother responding to the text, instead walking out to the adoption office where I find her entering information into the computer. Jade, one of the employees in the adoption office, sees me and smirks as I lean against the door frame. We've known each other since grade school. She lifts her head to properly meet my gaze and starts to speak but I shake my head at her, lifting a finger to my lips. Jade stifles a laugh when she realizes I'm waiting for Fallon to register my presence. Unsurprisingly, Marlow is the first of the two to notice, his big fluffy body jumping on me as he begs for attention. The movement finally catches Fallon's attention, her mouth forming a sexy as hell 'O' in surprise.

"Hi, Darlin'." I smirk at her as I bend down to say hello to her boy.

"What are you doing here?" She gasps before she turns back to the computer and pressing a few more keys. She locks the computer and stands up, walking over to me.

"I brought you something and wanted to offer my assistance." I grin at her, gesturing for her to follow me back to her office. "Go on, I won't bite," I give her a crooked smile. "Unless you want me to."

"Ryker," she warns, but her voice is more playful than annoyed.

"Just move it, beautiful" I chuckle, as I stifle an overwhelming need to playfully slap her ass as she walks ahead of me. I bite my knuckles to keep from acting on the desire as I follow her back to her office.

Marlow beats us back to her office and has somehow climbed onto the office chair which is now rolling across the floor. Fallon jogs over to stop him from crashing into anything, giggling at what just happened. Meanwhile, I'm trying to hold back a groan from the way her shorts are riding up her thighs from the short jog. The creamy expanse of her thick legs has my dick throbbing and pressing painfully against my zipper. I quickly adjust myself before she turns back to face me.

"Ok, we're here. Now, what did you need?" She's got that faux attitude again. I can't help the smile that dances on my lips. "I wanted to make sure you had lunch. Jake may have offered to take care of the rest of the day's tasks so I could come by and help however you need for the event this weekend."

"And why would Jake offer to do that?" She arches a brow at me, silently calling me out on my bullshit.

"Because I told him he was going to," I shrug as I step toward the food I left on her desk. "I also brought my second favorite fluff-butt a pup cake. I'd say favorite but you'll need to come over to meet Mr. Feeny to understand why that's just not possible." My smile widens when Marlow saunters over to me like he's king of the world.

"You're unbelievable," she sighs, as she moves the chair back to her desk and takes a seat. "I didn't need you to bring me lunch, I would have just grabbed something."

"Darlin', that's a crock of shit and you know it. Elle said you haven't had lunch for the past two weeks." I sit down across from her and open the box of pizza. "You need to eat, and you need a volunteer to take some things off your plate." I slide the box in her direction, smirking. "And would you look at that, I can help you out with both those things." A soft chuckle escapes from my lips when I hear her stomach growl.

Chapter Nine

Fallon

My anger is being defused by the scent of the pizza. Whoever came up with the idea of chicken parm pizza is a genius, and I will take a bullet for them if anyone says otherwise. Ryker is just staring at me while I'm nibbling on a slice. It's kind of unnerving, maybe more than kind of.

"Why are you watching me eat?" I roll my eyes when I see the smirk playing on his lips.

"I'm not watching you eat. I'm just hanging out, spending some time with a beautiful woman that I can't get enough of." The tone of his voice is playful, but the look in his eye is full of heat and desire.

I choke on my pizza at his response, doubling over in my chair as a violent cough claws up my throat. I struggle to catch my breath, and Ryker is on his feet, patting me on the back before I can push him away.

Finally, my breathing is under control and the pizza has gone down. I take a few deep inhales before I respond.

"It's never going to happen," I try my best to send a glare at the man before me.

"Aww, never say never, Darlin'," he flashes his panty dropping smile at me, which only pisses me off more. "Now, what can I do to help you?" He doesn't bother letting me speak before he snatches my to-do list from the desk.

Yes, I have a handwritten to-do list. What of it?

"Oh, for Christ's sake," I groan and stand, pacing back and forth as he takes the reins.

"Tents, tables, chairs. Food and drinks for volunteers and animals." He pauses and glances up at me. "What about food for those who come out to see the animals?"

My eyes go wide as I realize I completely forgot to book food for the attendees. "I hadn't discussed that with Fannie, but it's too late for anything like that now." I sigh, rubbing my temples as the weight of the event bears down on me. "I'll have to make sure to order some for the next event. I'm hoping to have a bigger one in the fall." Shit, I can't believe I dropped the ball on this.

"I'll take care of it," Ryker smiles as he continues reading down the list.

"What do you mean? Take care of *what*?" I blink at him in confusion.

"Exactly what I said." That shit eating grin is back on his face, sending my blood pressure soaring. "I'll get the tents, tables, and chairs. I have some at home. That way you don't have to buy anything. Use the money you save there to order food and drinks for the people attending. " Ryker looks so pleased with himself as he continues, "I'll drop them off with

Fannie after they close tomorrow night, and I'll come early to help set up."

"Ryker, stop it. You can't do all of this," I groan.

"Fallon, I want to help," He walks to where I stand, stepping into my space and forcing me backward into the wall. Again. He leans in so close I can smell the sweet yet masculine scent of his sweat. My breath hitches once his face is right in front of mine, my body stiff with anticipation. I'm not ready for whatever it is he's going to do, even if part of me wants anything he's willing to give me. A soft whimper leaves my lips when I feel his fingers grazing my sides. The corner of his lips twitch and he tilts his head, "Let me." A sudden knock at the door startles us both and Ryker drops his head to my shoulder, groaning.

"Yes?" It comes out all breathy as I step away, putting some much-needed distance between us.

The door opens and Shelby walks in, "Oh, oh my!" She giggles, obviously reading the room. "Hey, Fallon. Ryker. I didn't mean to interrupt."

"No, you're fine. What's up?" I ask, trying to slow my heart rate.

"Hey Shel, later Shel," Ryker waves at her before he lowers his head back to my ear, "I will see you later so we can continue our discussion." He crosses the space to the door and is gone before I can even attempt to respond.

My attention is focused on Shelby who has a wild grin on her face.

"Oh, you're totally gonna bone him!" She's giggling like a maniac.

"I am not!" I argue.

"Fallon, it's a small town, most of us grew up together. I'm not sure what I just walked in on, but I can promise you, I've not seen that man interested in anyone since high school when he dated Lexi." Her smile hasn't wavered, "it's only a matter of time before you give in."

"What happened with Lexi?" The question is out of my mouth before I can stop it. I knew it. There's always a catch.

"She and her family moved away when we were going into our junior year." She shrugs, "Not much of a story. Anyway! I'm here to see if we have any decorations to take to Woof 'n Tails yet. Fannie is so excited! I was just there, and she said we could start setting up the indoor sections immediately."

"Really?" I don't bother hiding my excitement. "That would be amazing! Yes, I have a few boxes here." I lead her to where I've been keeping everything I've purchased in the corner of my office.

"Great! I'll head back over in a bit. My husband just got back from a haul, so I'll have him help!" She smiles and wraps an arm around my shoulders. "This is going to be amazing!"

I flop back on my chair, my eyes shining with unshed tears. There are so many incredible people ready to help all these animals, to help me. Marlow comes running to me as soon as he senses that I'm overwhelmed with emotion. He jumps up to partially lay in my lap and I bury my face in his fur.

"Thanks, buddy, I'm ok." I smile through the tears. "It's good emotions, Macho Man. I promise." We stay like that for a bit before he feels confident enough to leave me alone. He grunts at me before flopping back down into his bed.

My afternoon goes by in a flash. Apparently, eating helps the time move faster and makes me more productive. With Ryker insisting he takes some things off my to do list, and Shelby coming by to grab decorations, it feels like a weight has been lifted off my shoulders. I've finalized the list of animals and volunteers, tomorrow will be spent spamming all corners of the internet with reminders of the event and securing food for everyone. Then it's just a matter of counting down the hours until the big event.

I sit up straight, stretching out my stiff body. I groan when I see it's already five and I haven't left yet. Shocked that Elektra hasn't called me to see where I am, I grab my phone as I stand. Marlow is on his feet as soon as I am. Once I find her contact, I press the call button, it only rings once.

Instead of a standard greeting of *Hello*, she answers saying "Bestie Boo, if Ryker hadn't told me how much crap you had on that to-do list, I would have come searching for you."

A chuckle bursts from my mouth, "I'm kind of glad he told you then. I'm just about to leave."

"Perfect, I'm on my way to get you, you're coming with me. See you in five." She disconnects the call.

Well, ok then.

Chapter Ten

My back porch leads down to a large, partially covered patio. Tables and chairs are spread out over the brick pavers, offering a variety of seating options while the smoker we bought last year stands off to one side. Momma insists on still hosting barbecues here even though she and my dad moved out a few years after he retired. She's made it a point to make sure any outdoor cooking appliance is here for me to use when she tells me the next party is scheduled.

The longer I go without dating, the pushier she gets about hosting opportunities where I can meet someone. I'm curious what her response will be when she meets Fallon. A vision of a future with the dark-haired beauty in this space makes my heart hammer a bit harder in my chest. Fallon setting out a cold dish of cut up watermelon, her denim shorts riding up her thighs…now that's a sight I could get used to. A wide grin splits my face when I hear Elle's car coming up the gravel drive. She parks next to my truck, as usual, but instead of just one car door closing, I hear two, along with a deep bark. I spot Marlow bounding around the corner just as I see two women come behind him.

"Hey buddy!" I kneel down, giving him the affection he's looking for. I glance back up just as Elle and Fallon join us on the patio.

"I brought you a surprise," Elle's sing-song voice is the one to break the silence.

"This is why you're my favorite pain in the ass, kiddo." I wink at her, as she groans.

"I'll take her home if you call me kiddo again," Elle makes herself at home and walks into my house, presumably to grab a drink.

"Hi, I'm guessing I'm the surprise? Although, with all the help you're giving me for the event, I'm not going to complain about that right now," Fallon's shy smile has all the blood pulsing through my veins rushing straight to my dick.

"Hi, Darlin'," I stand to my feet and take a few steps in her direction until I'm towering over her. My arms wrap around her delectable curves as my hands rest on the small of her back. She's stiff for a moment before she finally melts into me. Her arms loop around my waist holding onto me tighter than I think even she realizes.

"Hi, Ry." There is a lightness to her that I haven't heard before. Surprised at her use of my nickname, I pull back just enough to glance down at her, her eyes already on mine when I lean in, tilting her chin just a tad higher.

"Aw, this is cute and all, but can you get my man to come out while you're cooking?" Elle chimes in from behind us. Never in my life have I wanted to throttle her as much as I do right now.

"I hate you, so much more than usual right now, Elle." I growl at her, I lean back down and press my lips to Fallon's hair. I hear a sharp intake of air before stepping away from her. "Is Marlow going to be ok around a fox?"

"Uh, as long as it's friendly, I don't see why he wouldn't be ok." She snaps her fingers to have Marlow sit down next to her.

"Mr. Feeny! Fe – he – he – he – heeeeneeyyyy!" I yell out into the open space behind my house. I hear a gasp from behind me and turn to see the fluffy red fox rubbing on Marlow who has a furry brow raised, confused as to what this animal is. I chuckle, "Fallon, Marlow. This is Mr. Feeny."

"Oh my god." Fallon tries to keep her voice calm, but I can see the excitement vibrating through her sexy body. "Aren't you the most handsome fox ever!" She extends her hand for him to sniff, waiting patiently until he decides she can pet him, but the crazy ass that he is bypasses her hand and just leaps up into her chest. She squeals, her arms coming up quickly to hold him tightly.

Elle is at my side in a matter of seconds, and I glance over to see a sly smile on her face.

"I'll take Marlow for a walk. Make your move, ask her on a real date." She whispers while rolling her eyes at me, "Mr. Feeny has her right where you want her. Don't fuck it up."

A soft chuckle escapes me as she calls for Marlow's attention, which he gladly gives her. They run off together in the large freshly mowed yard. Elle's voice becomes fainter as they go past a row of trees that separates the yard from the patches.

"How do you feel about blackened chicken and Cajun garlic green beans?" I ask as I watch Fallon love on my fox. Mr. Feeney soaks up all the affection, acting as though the girl holding him is the only one to ever show him any. Would it be silly to admit I was jealous of a fox?

"What? You're cooking?" She asks, taking in her surroundings for the first time. She notices the Blackstone and her eyes go wide. "Ryker, you don't have to cook for us. I didn't even know she was bringing me here." She tries to argue, but I hold up a hand, silencing her.

"Woman," I chuckle, "Let me take care of you."

"I appreciate it but –," I step toward her and lift her gaze to mine.

"Fallon, I don't know what made you feel like you can't or shouldn't allow anyone in." My thumb caresses her cheek as I continue. "I promise you; I only want to make you happy."

She lets out a long breath and her eyes flutter closed as she finally leans into my touch.

"I'm going to make you dinner on Saturday, after the event. Just us, and Marlow." Her eyes go wide, and she opens her mouth to speak, but I cut her off. "Don't argue with me, it's a date." I wink before stepping away as I notice Elle and Marlow coming back from their too short walk.

"Dude, is dinner ready yet?" Elle collapses in one of the chairs around the unlit fire pit. "I'm starving."

"You know, you could offer to help. What would your Gran say if she saw you flopping down and making demands?" I tease her with a playful glare.

"She'd say good job, make the man do the work." She quips back, sticking her tongue out at me.

"Ugh, again, why do I put up with you?" I groan before stepping around Fallon who is trying unsuccessfully to hide her giggles.

"Because I got your girl here." Elle's response is so quick I can't help the deep rumble of laughter that escapes me.

"Speaking of the girl," Fallon joins in on the conversation. "Where can I get a drink?"

There's no time for me to respond or offer to take her inside to show her, Elle is on her feet with her arm looped through Fallon's as she leads her into the house. I notice Fallon looking over her shoulder at me with a shy smile. A smug grin starts to form when she looks back quickly, knowing I caught her.

Chapter Eleven

The bed had just been delivered a week ago. We've both been so tired we haven't even had a chance to break it in ourselves, and yet I get home early to find Kyle railing Ruth from behind. I've never seen the man move this fast in my life. She's screaming his name on repeat praying to the heavens that he doesn't stop. I'm going to be sick.

It's been nearly a year since I found them in our bed. So why is that the first thing that flashes through my mind when I'm asked on a date by someone new? Ok, maybe I wasn't asked, per se, but I know I haven't been making this easy for him. Elle leads me into the kitchen of Ryker's house, and when I turn to her, my face must show the anxiety I'm feeling.

"Whoa, Bestie Boo, what is it?" Her hands are linked with mine, immediately trying to calm me down.

"He wants me to come over on Saturday after the event so he can make me dinner. He said it was a date." My breaths start coming faster and faster, my chest tightening. "He said it's a date. Elle, I don't I – I don't know if I can..." the words die on my lips.

"Fallon, I'm going to tell you a secret." Her eyes are full of love and kindness. "I know you got fucked over in the worst kind of way, but if anyone is going to prove to you that they're worth taking a risk. It's Ryker."

I'm unable to respond, my heart smashing against my rib cage as it threatens to burst from my chest.

"He may be a pain in the ass with me, but I've not seen him this smitten in ages. He's not going to string you along and he'd *never* cheat on you. I can guarantee that." She seems so sure of him, it's almost disarming. "Also, I kind of like Elle better, Elektra is such a mouth full."

I snort. "Why didn't you say something sooner?"

"Eh, I'm not one to rock the boat." She shrugs. "It's just a name, but since you shortened it now, you gave me an opening. So, thanks!"

I'm laughing, my anxiety temporarily forgotten, as she opens the door to grab my drink. Once it's closed, she hands me a bottle of water before looping her arm back through mine. We walk back out to the patio to join Ryker, who has our dinner plated and waiting on a farmhouse style round table. The evening sky is just starting to darken as the sun fades off into the horizon.

"Wow." It comes out in a whispered tone as I finally get a chance to take in the view. Ryker has an adorable set up with seating and tables spread across the large patio area. A row of tall fluffy trees lines the far side of the yard. It's so open and peaceful here. "I didn't realize how beautiful this place is."

"Between the fox and the man meat, I get it." Elektra – er – Elle … that's going to take some getting used to – responds like the sarcastic bundle of energy she is.

"Did you just call me 'man meat'?" Ryker asks with a fork full of green beans halfway to his lips.

"Sure did, Ry! Whatcha gonna do about it?" She teases him.

"My god, you two really are like siblings," I can't help the laughter that bubbles from my chest.

The rest of the evening continues without any further awkwardness. Ryker makes it a point to touch me any chance he gets, and I can't say I'm mad about it. The lightest caresses remind me he's there and thinking about me. My body is humming from the tease of connection he's been giving me all night. The sun is long gone by the time Elle stands up and declares it's time to go.

"You don't have to go, Elle." Ryker yawns.

"Am I the only one who remembers you wake up at four to get everything done at the farm? That's why we only do this once a week." I can practically hear her eyes roll from where I'm sitting, "You'll see her tomorrow."

I stand, guilt making me move quickly so we can let Ry get some sleep. "If I knew you woke up that early, I would have left much earlier."

"Which is exactly why I didn't mention it, Darlin'," Ryker teases while another yawn escapes.

"We'll see you tomorrow, go to bed." Elle waves him toward his house as she stands and motions for Marlow to follow her to give us some space, which he does. *Traitor.*

Ryker is on his feet, looming over me in a flash. Keeping his eyes on me, I feel him gesture something behind my back to Elle who laughs in the distance. My breathing picks up as he wraps an arm around my waist, holding me like he did before. But unlike earlier, he cups my cheek gently.

"As much as I want to kiss you, I'm going to be a gentleman and wait." His thumb lightly traces along my bottom lip, "For now."

Ryker drops his hand from my face and guides me back to where Elle parked. She has Marlow tucked into the car, strapped in with the doggy seatbelt she purchased shortly after she saw mine.

"Thank you for dinner." I meet Ryker's eyes again; we're staring at each other for what must be a while because Elle honks the horn, Marlow barking at the loud noise. Ryker and I chuckle before separating. "Goodnight."

"Goodnight, Darlin'," he winks before he turns to climb the stairs.

Elle is giddy when I climb into her car. She's buzzing with questions that I'm not prepared to answer. I don't want to get myself excited for something that I don't trust yet, especially when I'm still so damaged. Do I even *want* to be with Ryker? My heart aches as I think of the unknown. The drive home goes by quickly, and as much as I love her, I'm so thankful to get some space from my friend. It's not that I don't want to talk to her, I just don't know what to say right now.

It's only nine-thirty, and I'm more than ready to climb into bed for the night. I pull my phone from my purse only to realize that the battery is dead. I toss it on the charger and give it some time to charge before I turn it back on. I know I won't wake up without the alarm set if I fall asleep when it's still off. Almost immediately, the screen lights up with a message notification.

Ryker:

Sweet dreams, beautiful. I'll be counting the moments until I see you in the morning.

Chapter Twelve

The blaring noise of the alarm jolts me out of an incredibly vivid dream. I groan into the emptiness of my bedroom. With a quick glance out my window, it's easy to see the moon is fading in the distance as the night slowly changes to morning. I stretch while still in bed, my limbs waking for the day.

The clock says it's just after four in the morning. My mind drifts off to Fallon as soon as my feet touch the floor. I grin at the memory of her being here last night, how she felt in my arms. She seemed to relax more with each innocent touch throughout the night.

The fragrance of fresh coffee brewing from my kitchen has me following the scent to find Jake in my house. I nod my head at him, not ready to speak yet. He's wearing his normal jeans, boots, and a short sleeve shirt, ready to start the workday. We tend to wear the same thing; the only real difference being the backwards Chicago White Sox cap covering his light blond hair and the cowboy hat covering mine. The man will survive on only an hour of sleep if it means he doesn't miss a game. He grunts when he hands me a mug of black coffee and once I have the steaming cup in my hands, I take a long sip.

Now that I feel somewhat up to communicating with people once the liquid gold has entered my bloodstream, I glance up at my friend. Jake is leaning against my kitchen counter like he fucking lives here. "Why the hell are you in my house already?"

He furrows his brow, "you texted me last night after nine saying to just come in and start the coffee because you'd be moving slower today." I slide my phone out of my pocket to see I did, in fact, text him.

"Shit, I was so tired. I don't remember even sending that." I admit, setting my cell on the table.

"The woman from the shelter?" An amused expression appears on his face.

"Fallon and Elle," I yawn.

"Ah, next time let me know. I'll keep Elle distracted for you," Jake's green eyes twinkle with mischief.

"Marlow kept her distracted enough that we were able to have a moment." My lips tip up into a bright smile, "she's coming over tomorrow after the adoption event. I'm gonna make her dinner."

"Who's Marlow?" Jake's eyes have turned dark.

"Huh?" I'm taken off guard by the question. "Oh, it's Fallon's golden retriever."

He nods, not sharing any further thoughts. A few minutes later my coffee is finished and I'm ready to tackle the day.

Once we're out in the fields, it appears that one patch has become overgrown with weeds within the last day. Jake spends a generous amount of time gently pulling them from around the pumpkin vines. Meanwhile, I've got tons of mulch that needs to be spread out. It's close to seven when I realize I'm not going to make it to the shop for Fallon's morning coffee run. I pull my phone from my pocket and send a text to Elle, letting her know I'll stop by this afternoon to pay for Fallon's caffeine fix. I debate sending another message to Fallon, but since I don't know what time she wakes up and I don't usually see her until after eight a.m. most days, I decide against it for now. I'll check in on her later.

Before long, the sun is high in the sky, beads of sweat drip down my skin as heat beats down on my back. I lift the cowboy hat I've had for years off my head and wipe my brow, panting from the oppressive humidity. Grateful to finally have the last of the day's chores done, I send Jake on his way so I can wash up before I head into town. I make it the quickest shower of my life and end up at Elle's just after noon.

"Tell me you texted her," my oldest friend greets me as soon as I enter The Caffeinated Pumpkin.

"Good morning to you too, Elle. And yes, I texted her last night, why?" I'm confused as I watch her slap her face with an incredibly dramatic face palm.

"You text another woman that you won't be able to see the woman you've been trying to go out with for a minute, right? Why would you text me but not her?"

"But you're not another woman, you're just Elle." I shrug, still not seeing a problem. "And I didn't want her to have to pay for her coffee. I've been planning on seeing her for lunch once the chores were done."

"You're such a dumb boy. Take this," she pushed a coffee in my direction. "Go get her lunch and pray she's not big mad. She missed you this morning. And when she realized you texted me and not her, she looked hurt. It's not that you text me, it's that you didn't text her." She rolls her eyes and shoos me away.

I climb back in my truck and grab a couple of burgers from the diner before I head over to the shelter.

After I park, I climb out of the truck and walk with purpose to the door. I'm able to get back to her office again with ease. It's not lost on me that no one speaks to me on my way through the building. I push the door open to see her on her computer with Marlow at her side. A calmness takes over when my eyes land on her. She doesn't notice me at first, it's not until Marlow grunts and his tail thumps against the floor that her gaze meets mine. Her face lights up with what looks like relief. Huh.

"Hey, beautiful." I grin at her. "I'm sorry I didn't get a chance to swing by the shop this morning. But you didn't think I'd be able to make it the whole day without you, did you, Darlin'?"

Her eyes glisten with unshed tears. "I thought it was some sort of elaborate joke, you pushing so hard to get me to go out with you just to drop me." She chokes out a forced laugh and shakes her head, covering her face with her hands. "It wouldn't be the first time."

I close the distance between us and drop to my knees in front of her. Gently, I pull her hands away before cupping her cheeks, forcing her to hold my gaze. "Nothing about this is a joke," I lean in to press my lips against hers to show her how serious I am when Marlow pushes me away and knocks my ass onto the ground before our mouths can connect and someone walks into her office clearing their throat. "Son of a bitch." I grumble under my breath which makes her giggle. And it is the most beautiful sound.

Chapter Thirteen

Fallon

Yesterday, Ryker refused to leave my side for the rest of the afternoon. It was sweet, even if it wasn't necessary. I'm confident we have everything we could possibly need for today. My heart is racing with anxiety and excitement. It's only seven a.m. but I can't sleep anymore. I climb out of bed and grab my phone to see a text from Elektra that came through about an hour ago.

> Good morning, my beautiful Bestie Boo bundle of joy. It's event day! Are you ready? Of course you're ready!. Do you need anything from me? Besides coffee, obviously, you need my coffee. No, really. Let me know when you're awake and I'll be right up with the biggest mug of coffee you've ever seen.

Fallon:

> How is it possible you have so many things to say before seven in the morning? And on a Saturday of all days?

Elle:

> Aww, you're such a grumpy gill. I'll be right up with your piping hot, happy bean juice.

Not even two minutes later she's strolling into my bedroom just as I walk out of my connected bathroom. I glare at her as she holds out a large mug the size of her head toward me, a bright and slightly irritating smile plastered on her face.

"Are you ok?" I ask, "You're starting to frighten me." I admit as I take a sip of coffee.

The profile of flavors burst on my tongue, and I moan as I swallow that first gulp. It's truly heaven. Elle is staring at me, waiting for permission to speak again. I snort before I wave my hand for her to continue.

"I'm just really excited for your day!" Elle beams, bouncing slightly. "Plus, I know Ryker has plans for you guys tonight and I can't wait to hear what he does. I've never seen him put this kind of effort into a woman before." I shake my head as she rambles, sitting on the edge of the bed.

"Thank you," I smirk. "Can I get your opinion on what I'm planning to wear tonight? I'm going to stop by here to change and get Marlow before I head to Ry's place."

"Oh my god, yes!" She squeals, clapping her hands together excitedly.

I pull out a deep green sun dress that hugs my curves in the most flattering way. Her eyes bug out of her head when she sees it on the hanger. I can't help but chuckle.

"You think he'll like it?" I ask hopefully.

"Bestie, if he doesn't lose his mind when he sees you in that dress, I'm taking him to get his head checked." She dramatically fans her face with her hand.

"Thank you for that." I smile at her. "For everything," I pause for a moment, apprehension swirling in my gut. "I'm afraid..." I whisper the admission.

"Bestie, what exactly are you afraid of?" Elle's directness forces me to say it out loud.

"Kyle and Ruth," I say quietly and she makes a face.

"Eww, he's like my brother. Even the thought," Elle shudders dramatically. "That's soooo gross."

We're both laughing at her reaction when my phone vibrates with a text.

Ryker:

> Good morning, Darlin', I hope I'm not waking you.

I smile at the message when Elle's phone goes off a second later. She looks at her screen and snorts. She shows me the screen with a message from Ryker.

Do you mind if I hang out at your place until she wakes up?

She doesn't give me a chance to respond to him before she presses the call icon, putting her finger in front of her lips to tell me to stay quiet. The line rings briefly, and she presses the speaker button just as he answers.

"Hey, kiddo." His deep voice fills the room, smooth like a barrel aged bourbon.

"You're already sitting outside, aren't you?" She asks him.

"I might be." He chuckles sheepishly, like a kid that's just been caught doing something they shouldn't be.

"Why don't you just come upstairs, she's drinking coffee and about to get dressed. Although, I could probably hold her off on the clothes if you hurry." She smirks, waggling her eyebrows up and down.

"You have me on speaker, don't you?"

"I might..." She repeats his words from a second ago.

"Fucking hell, Elle." He groans. "Good morning, Darlin'.'"

I let out the giggle I've been holding in since she first dialed him.

"Come on up, Ry. I'm sure Elle left the door unlocked." I snort before pushing off the bed to find my clothes for the event.

Ryker and I pull up to Woof 'n Tails thirty minutes later with a thermos of freshly brewed coffee and a sausage egg and cheese burrito that Elle insisted I take. Meanwhile, Ryker asked for a burrito and was told he should have eaten before he left this morning. He claims he did eat, but he's a growing boy and needs a second breakfast, drawing a laugh from deep in my chest. I let out a heavy sigh and before I turn to open the door, Ryker startles me by grabbing my hand. My gaze meets his; the anxiety rolling from me in waves must be obvious with how he's looking at me.

"Darlin,' it's going to be an amazing day. I'm going to be here, and you have an incredible team of volunteers." He cups my cheek in his hand, and I nod silently before opening the door to slide out.

We make quick work of setting up the tables and crates for the cats to be placed in until someone, hopefully, adopts them. Ryker has the tents popped up in a matter of minutes, surprising the hell out of me. He tells me how they use them at the farm several times a year for various events, explaining how he can maneuver them with such ease.

Volunteers begin to arrive around nine to help with last minute setup. I've been posting images on our social media accounts all morning to show what the *behind the scenes* looks like to make people feel more involved and encourage them to come out.

"Fallon!" Shelby hollers from across the parking lot.

I wave to her before jogging over to meet her. "Hey, what's up?"

"I just wanted to let you know that we have ten cats inside already and the fosters with the dogs are on their way," she announces, having taken over as my second in command so I could catch my breath over the last two days. "A handful of volunteers are also bringing the dogs from the shelter to meet potential adopters."

"That's incredible! Thank you!" She's really been doing a great job, and I genuinely appreciate all her help.

The event itself only lasts for four hours. Ryker really outdid himself. I didn't know what to expect when he said he'd take care of it a couple of days ago, but when I saw the grill my heart melted a little more. The man stood over a hot grill for three hours to make sure everyone that wanted one got a hot dog and he even brought snack bags of chips to hand out.

The final number of adoptions for the day has my heart feeling fuller than I expected. Not only did all of the cats get adopted, but twelve of the fifteen dogs that were brought out now have forever homes, too. Shelby's happy tears match my own when she comes over to say goodbye after we get everything packed up. I haven't been able to talk to Ryker most of the day, so when he approaches me to see my tear-stained cheeks his face falls.

"Darlin'?" He stands in front of me, concern etched across his handsome features. "What's wrong?"

"Absolutely nothing," I say, covering his hands with mine. "Today went better than I ever could have dreamed."

I smile proudly at him.

Ryker

I pull up to my house shortly after dropping Fallon off at her place to shower and pick up Marlow. She insisted on driving herself here, and usually I'd argue, but I did want to shower and change before she got here. I'll save that argument for another time. I rush inside and run up to the bathroom. After I turn the shower on, I undress and toss my clothes in the hamper. The water heats up quickly, which feels so good on my sore muscles. I'm used to the feeling, but today it's more noticeable since I was standing in one spot at the grill for so long. I grab my loofa from the hook on the shower wall and let the hot water saturate the netting. With a few pumps of body wash on my loofa, I lather up, swiftly washing my sweat covered body.

Once the day's chores and work are washed from my skin, I manscape. Not to be presumptuous, but I also don't want to be ill-prepared for whatever may happen. I try to be a gentleman after all, even if I'd do anything for a taste. Once I finish up in the shower, I step out and dry off, reaching for my jeans that I had left on my bed. I hear the sound of gravel crunching under tires so I grab my shirt before rushing to meet her.

Fallon pulls up just as I walk back downstairs. I step out onto the porch as I tug a white T-shirt over my head. Her eyes are wide, the low light from inside the car letting me see her through the windshield. I can't help but smirk, realizing she was stunned to see my bare chest, even for a second. She's out of the car in a flash, Marlow trotting close behind her.

"Hey, beau –," the words die on my tongue. There isn't an adjective strong enough to describe the breathtaking sight before me.

Deep green material stretches over every dip and curve of her body, and I can't keep my eyes from raking over every inch as she approaches. The flowy sleeves fall off the shoulders, showing off just enough skin that I'm aching to explore every exposed bit of flesh with my tongue. She smiles nervously as I take her in. Her hair is styled in loose waves, the lightest layer of makeup giving her a gorgeous glow in the sunset light. My heart hammers in my chest; there is nothing in this world that can top how stunning she looks right now.

"Wow," I try to speak again. "Darlin', there aren't enough words in the English language to describe how beautiful you are. You're fucking perfect." I breathe as I take a step closer to her and wrap her tightly in my arms. My hand finds her cheek and I lean down to kiss her when the Marco's Pizza delivery driver pulls up and honks.

"What on earth did I do in a former life to be interrupted every fucking time?" I groan.

A kid from town, Corbin, steps out with a couple of pizzas. "Hey Mr. Addams, I have your food!" He's completely oblivious to the Olympic-sized wrench he just threw into my mojo as he steps up to the porch. I drop my arms from around Fallon and take the pizzas from him.

"Thanks, Corbin," I nod at him.

"You're welcome. Hey, since I'm here, my parents have been talking about the pumpkin festival." The kid smiles, I can't tell if he's fucking with me and intentionally cockblocking me or if he is really that damn unaware. "Have you decided how many entries you'll take for the best pumpkin pie?"

"I haven't, we'll be doing some different things with the festival this year. I'll be sure to get the event page updated once we decide." I chuckle, "Momma still likes to be involved, even if they aren't part of the day to day anymore."

He nods and waves before he climbs back into his car and drives off.

"I wanted to cook but after manning the grill all day, I figured we could do pizza." I explain, "I got you chicken parm again."

Fallon shoots me an appreciative smile. "Pizza is perfect. I'm all in for a relaxing night." She muses.

I guide her and Marlow around to the back patio and we dig in. She gets through a slice of pizza before she declares she's full. I arch a brow at her and she giggles.
"Ok fine, I'll have one more slice."

"Good girl." I smirk and her cheeks flush a beautiful pink at the praise. "That's good to know." I chuckle darkly.

"Hmm?" She asks as she's chewing.

"Oh, nothing at all, Darlin'." I'm going to hold that information to use later.

Don't worry, I'll only use the power for good.

I watch while she continues eating. Once she finishes the second slice she leans back, a satisfied sigh leaving her lips. I hold my hand out to her to help her up, her fingers sliding delicately along my palm. She follows me to the porch swing and curls up by my side as we watch the stars.

"How are you feeling after today?" I ask her, my own excitement is still radiating through my body, and I was just there to help.

"I feel wonderful, overwhelmed, thankful." she ticks off the emotions she's processing.

I smile to myself and hold her tighter to my side. We chat about the basics, not ready to push into anything too deep just yet. I hear a contented sigh, but she doesn't answer my last question – does she have any siblings? Suddenly, her breathing deepens and I feel the steady rise and fall of her chest. I chuckle quietly when I glance down at the gorgeous creature in my arms to find she's fast asleep.

As gently as possible, I stand to my feet and lift Fallon into my arms to carry her inside. I do my best not to jostle her as I walk into the house. Thankfully, I've had to get the screen door open with no hands before, I know the trick to getting in without waking her. I dig the toe of my boot into the wood embellishment that sticks out a bit from the screen and pull the door open. I click my tongue for Marlow to follow and he pads inside. I carry her inside to my bedroom. As much as I should be a gentleman in this situation, I can't bring myself to leave her. Holding her tightly to me, I bend slightly and pull the blankets back. She barely stirs when I lay her on the bed. I yank my white t-shirt over my head and methodically dress and undress her at once. I may plan on sharing a bed with her tonight, but I have no intention of seeing her naked until she's awake and can give me the green light.

Once she's fully covered in my shirt and I have her dress hanging on the closet door, I shuck off my dark blue Wranglers and lay them on the armchair next to my window. Then after I climb into bed behind her, I pull the blankets on top of us. I wrap one arm over her middle, the other tucked under my head as I pull her closer, her back pressed flush to my chest. I smile into her hair at our closeness and press a soft kiss to the sensitive spot where her neck meets her shoulder. Fallon lets out a soft moan in her sleep at the intimate connection.

I close my eyes, a peace I've never experienced in my life settling deep in my soul.

Chapter Fifteen

Fallon

A bright light streams in from the window, and I groan at the interruption to my sleep. I roll over to wrap an arm around the furry neck that's always sharing my pillow, only to find Marlow's not here. My eyes shoot open, and I look around the room, quickly realizing I'm not in my own bed. That explains why the sun's rays are coming in; I always make sure my blinds are closed before bed. Shit, I fell asleep at Ryker's house.

Memories of a wonderful time with the beautiful man that I have been trying to fight off come swirling back in my foggy mind. How did I end up in his bed? The last thing I remember is star gazing on the porch swing, crap. A startled gasp leaves my lips when I look down to see I'm in his T-shirt. We didn't? No. I don't feel like I've had sex. I still have my bra and panties on. I wouldn't have gotten dressed again if we had.

As much as I'm not a fan of mornings, I feel surprisingly well rested this morning. I climb to my feet and pad out of the room when I get a whiff of bacon. I follow the scent down the stairs to find Ryker standing at the stove making an elaborate breakfast of bacon, sausage, eggs, pancakes... holy shit, are those fried potatoes? And a fruit salad? Am I dreaming? Unable to conceal my surprise at seeing him preparing such an elaborate breakfast, a small gasp breaks free.

Hearing me, Ryker glances over his shoulder, a beautiful, wide smile splits his face, "Good mornin', Darlin'."

He crosses the distance in two long strides and cups the back of my head, his fingers tangling into my hair. I gasp at the bold move as he lowers his face to mine. I close my eyes and feel his breath against my lips just as an excited shriek startles us apart.

"Oh, my goodness, Ryker! You're seeing someone?" A small, older woman is standing in the doorway, clapping her hands wildly as she looks between the two of us. Ryker presses his forehead against mine with an exasperated sigh, closing his eyes in frustration.

"Hi, Momma." He groans, "I love you and all but for the love of God, can you knock next time?"

"Oh hush, child." She waves him off before turning her attention to me. "Hi sweetheart, I'm Colleen Addams, Ryker's momma. It's so nice to meet you!"

"Hi Mrs. Addams, I'm Fallon. It's nice to meet you too." I smile shyly, suddenly feeling more insecure about the fact that I'm in nothing but her son's shirt. "I'm um, I'm going to go get dressed."

"Mrs. Addams was my mother-in-law, and I absolutely adored the woman, but please call me Colleen, or better yet, Momma." She responds as I slowly back out of the kitchen.

I rush upstairs and find my dress hanging on the closet door. After I strip out of Ryker's shirt, I pull on my dress from last night. Instantly missing the scent of him around me, I sigh. My phone lights up on the bedside table and I quickly grab it to see a message from Elle.

Elle:

Where are you? It's eight a.m. Did you get some last night?

Fallon:

No! We haven't even kissed, I just fell asleep, and he put me to bed. I went downstairs this morning, and he tried to kiss me, but his mom came in!

Elle:

Aw! Momma Addams is there?

Fallon:

Yes! I don't know what to do, I have to go downstairs in the same clothes from last night.

Elle:

Wait, what were you wearing when she came in?

Fallon:

He dressed me in one of his T-shirts when I passed out. That's not the point! I'm doing a walk of shame in front of his mother!

Elle:

Bestie Boo, it's not a walk of shame if you didn't get laid. Besides, Momma Addams is probably just ecstatic to know he's not a total recluse.

I take a deep breath and lock my phone, shoving it into the pocket of my dress – yes, it has pockets – before heading downstairs. *It's fine, I'm fine, I can totally do this.* Colleen and Ryker are sitting at the table chatting when I enter the kitchen. His eyes find me immediately and a wicked smirk plays at his lips.

Ryker is on his feet, pulling out a chair for me to sit down next to him before I even make it to the table. I hesitantly take the seat, and he hands me a plate piled high with food. My god, it smells delicious. Ryker places a reassuring hand on my thigh, giving a light squeeze, just as his mother turns to me.

"Tell me everything! How did you meet? Where are you from, you're not from around here are you? What do you do?" Colleen bombards me with questions all before I've even had a sip of coffee.

Dear lord, please help me. Marlow's nails clack on the floor as he walks up next to me and lays his head on my other thigh grunting out his own expression of discomfort from the twenty questions so early in the morning. I quietly chuckle to myself before I steal Ryker's coffee from in front of him and take a sip. It's black and has no added flavor. Gross, but, hey, at least it's coffee.

"Momma! Give her a second, she just woke up right before you walked in." He groans, scrubbing his hand down his face. I glance up at him and smile softly, taking in the thick stubble. He's gorgeous. It really should be illegal to look so damn good, especially this early in the morning.

"It's fine." I place a hand on his forearm and lean into his side. "We met at The Caffeinated Pumpkin. I'm a sucker for pumpkin spice coffee and when I found out that Elle has it year-round, well, I was a goner. He was there a couple of weeks ago and has been bothering me ever since."

"You've enjoyed every second of me bothering you." He winks at me as he wraps an arm around the back of my chair, his fingers drawing gentle circles around the bare skin of my shoulder.

The moment I answer Colleen's last question, Elle bursts in the door.

"Where is she!?" She squeals before darting over to Colleen who she embraces and lifts to her feet.

"Oh child, you act like you haven't seen me in years. It's only been a month." She teases Elle.

"That's the longest I've gone without seeing you since we've met, Momma Addams." She dramatically replies, "No more cruises for you and Pops."

"I'll remember that when you want to go on a vacation." Her playful response makes my heart full.

"Just what in the hell are you doing here?" Ryker glares at Elle.

"What? I wanted breakfast and I figured," she says as she produces a tray of to-go cups, she must have placed them on the counter before hugging Colleen, "that Fallon would want coffee."

"...you're going to just need to give me some of the flavoring you make so I can keep it here for future mornings." Ryker grumbles.

"Ooooohhhhhh." Elle and Colleen taunt us.

"So you plan on more mornings together?" Colleen asks innocently.

My face heats and turns bright red with embarrassment as I bury my face in my hands. He chuckles and squeezes me closer into his side.

"You're both children." He throws back at the two women.

We spend a little while chatting with his mom and Elle over breakfast. Colleen makes it a point to share details about Ryker's childhood that have him cringing next to me and holding on to my thigh tighter, I'm guessing to make sure I don't run away. Never having had such an easy time talking to a parent of someone I'm dating—or shit, just in general –

I laugh at his reaction. It's ten in the morning by the time any of us check the clock and I excuse myself to head home. I need to go to change and run to the shelter to get everything put away before work tomorrow.

Ryker follows me out to my car and presses his forehead against mine, his hand cupping my cheek again as he glides his thumb over my bottom lip. My breath hitches, hoping he will finally kiss me. I tilt my face up to meet his, but he pulls away.

"Darlin', the first time I kiss you, it's not going to be quick and right now isn't the time to press you against your car so I can finally taste you." He groans, "No matter how badly I know we both want to."

I blink wildly when he steps away. What did I do in a past life to suffer through this constant clam jam since I met this man. *What the hell does a girl have to do to get kissed around here?*

Chapter Sixteen

I calmly walk back into my house, where I find my mother and Elle still chatting like nothing has happened. After pouring myself another cup of coffee, I set the mug on the table and flop down on the chair. I can feel their eyes on me, so I wave my hand in front of my face.

"Go on, get it all out so you don't embarrass her again," I roll my eyes at them.

My mother takes that as her green light and jumps right in. "I like her. She is exactly what you need." She has the biggest knowing grin on her face, and I groan.

"Are your lips broken?" Elle cuts in with a question I should have known to expect. I groan, ready for this inquisition to be over already.

"Elle!" My mother gasps in mock horror.

"What? He hasn't kissed her." She shrugs as she lifts a glass of water to her mouth.

"Trust me, it's not for lack of trying," I announce, admittedly a bit louder than necessary. "Because every damn time that I try, someone walks in and interrupts us!"

"Oh, oh my." Momma smirks, "That explains why you were so flustered with me when I got here. I'm so sorry, Ryker."

Elle says her goodbyes not long after. I spend the rest of the afternoon with my mother. She tells me about her and dad's cruise. Apparently, he caught something on the boat and is home resting. As much as I love my dad, it's nice to have some time with just Momma. We walk the grounds so she can see how the patches are growing this season. She's still so invested, even if she's no longer part of the day to day running of the property.

"Momma," I say as we're rounding the last green house. "What do you think of hosting an animal adoption event at the pumpkin fest this year? Fallon runs the shelter in town, and they just had an incredible turn out for a small event at Fannie's."

"Are you finally going to give me a grandbaby?" She asks, her tone completely serious. She has her hands planted on her hips in that I-mean-business way she did when I was younger.

"I'm sorry, what? I said animal adoption, Momma!" I croak out.

"I'm aware, you won't actually claim Mr. Feeny as a fur-baby, so are you going to adopt a dog?" She grins up at me. "But, to answer your question, I think that's a lovely idea. It will bring even more people out. I'll add that to my list, unless you would like to plan that portion with Fallon?"

"You're trying to kill me today, aren't you?" I sigh, "I'll talk to her about it and let you know."

Once we're back at the house she says her goodbyes, heading home to make my dad dinner. I let out a long breath, thankful to finally be alone.

I've been sitting on the porch swing enjoying the warm day, Mr. Feeny curled up in a ball next to me. I look down and chuckle realizing he looks so much like the Firefox icon. A need to snap a picture to send to Fallon comes over me. I grab my phone from my pocket, careful not to startle him. Her response comes shortly after I hit send on the picture.

Fallon:

> He's too cute, I can't wait to get more snuggles!

Ryker:

> From him or me? (wink emoji)

Fallon:

> Both, and Marlow, of course.

Ryker:

> I will make that happen.

Her response is a kiss and heart eyes emoji. My skin heats with a fire that I've been forced to push down for two weeks. The need is far too potent to ignore any longer. I glance at the time, it's already after six and I've got to be up at the ass crack of dawn.

Fuck it.

I walk inside my house and grab my keys from the hook by the door before rushing back out. My heart hammers in my chest, anxious about her reaction, but I can't find a reason to stop myself. She wanted it as badly as I did each time our lips nearly met, and I'll be damned if I'm going to deny her again. I race to her house, and make it in record time. Simultaneously patting myself on the back for how quickly I drove over while also scolding myself for being reckless.

The door to my truck is open before I shift into park, and I barely remember to close it once I jump out, before I'm climbing the steps to her apartment. I knock on the door like a nutcase and wait. Shit, what if she isn't here? I groan to myself for not texting her first, but then I hear Marlow bark. She's here, no way she'd leave him alone if she could help it. The door slowly opens a moment later to a beautiful dark-haired beauty with wide eyes. She's wearing a tiny, cropped tank top that barely covers her breasts, and the shortest pair of lounge shorts I've ever seen. My dick has been at half-mast since I decided to come over here, but now it's at full attention. Her eyebrows pull together as she silently questions what I'm doing, but before I can second guess myself, I pull her into my arms and crash my mouth to hers.

Fallon melts into me as my tongue delves between her lips, enjoying the sweet flavor of her. A soft moan escapes her when I suck on her bottom lip and bite gently. Her hands loop around my neck and her fingers dig into my scalp as she deepens the kiss even more. I hold her body flush against mine, feeling every dip and curve I possibly can from this angle and enjoying every second of her body on mine.

My hands wrap around her back, molding to the contours of her curves. I fight the urge not to sit her on the closest piece of furniture and take her right here. She whimpers into my mouth as I continue to devour her. The moment my hands are on her beautiful round ass I hear a throat clear, and a slow clap starts behind her. We both stiffen and I reluctantly pull away.

For the love of all things holy, why me?

Chapter Seventeen

I have never hated someone as much as I hate Elle right now. She's still slow-clapping behind us as I bury my face into Ryker's chest. He wraps an arm around my back, holding me against him. Whether it's to comfort me or hide the impressive erection he's hiding in his jeans is anyone's guess.

"It took you long enough, man." Elle giggles and skips back to her spot on the couch where we were watching Twilight and discussing who we want more as adults, Carlisle or Chief Swan.

Daddy Swan all the way.

"I didn't realize you were here," he directs to Elle, before leaning in closer to my ear and whispering. "I'm sorry for barging in, I just couldn't handle not knowing what you tasted like any longer."

"I'm not complaining." I smile up at him, my cheeks still tinged pink. "Do you want to stay and share which team you're on with us?" I tease him.

"Darlin', if I stay, Elle is leaving and neither of us will be working tomorrow." He says softly into my ear. Heat courses through my veins, and my body trembles with lust.

"I – um –," I'm unable to respond.

"I'll see you in the morning for coffee, beautiful." He presses his lips against mine in a chaste kiss before he disappears, closing the door behind him as he heads out to his truck.

"You are the worst person in the entire world, and I hate you with every fiber of my being." I groan to Elle who has a handful of popcorn halfway to her mouth, which Marlow decides is his when she stops moving.

"Hey, that's rude!" She's talking to both of us which diffuses my frustration a bit. She shrugs before saying, "he should have called first. It's not my fault we were in the middle of a serious discussion."

I pin her with a glare that should make her question her life choices, but it only seems to entertain her further.

"Plus, you can't hate me. I supply the coffee and without the coffee you can't do the word-putting into sentence-doing." She rattles off part of one of my favorite lines from the one and only Lorelai Gilmore.

"Just because you referenced Gilmore Girls, I'll forgive you." I pick up the remote and press play again.

I wake up to a loud crack of thunder, and a moment later, lightning flashes across the dark night sky. The heavens open, and a torrential downpour is released from above as the fat raindrops pound on the windows and roof. I glance at my phone to see it's only five. I groan, flopping back on my pillow, knowing I won't fall back asleep. I notice a message that wasn't there when I went to sleep.

Ryker:

> Good mornin', Darlin'. Be safe driving, it's supposed to be rough out there today. I'll bring your coffee to work so you don't have to get out of the car.

The message came through an hour ago. He must have messaged me as soon as he woke up. Why does this man have to make my insides feel all gooey? It's gross. I love it, but it's gross.

I send a quick response before rolling to Marlow who is snoring loudly next to me.

Fallon:

> My white knight. Thank you!

I last another twenty minutes in bed before I become too restless to try to get any more sleep. Marlow sprawls out and takes up the entire mattress the second I stand. "Love you too, bud." I roll my eyes at him before I head to the kitchen and grab a bottle of water from the fridge.

I spend a little extra time on my face today, even though I know the chances of it being ruined by the rain are pretty high. I'm not the biggest fan of foundation, since it always feels so heavy, so I apply a light layer of tinted moisturizer. Once that has set, I pull my bronzer and blush duo from the makeup bag and apply a little bit of both. It gives my face an entirely new look. My favorite eyeshadow palette needs to be replaced, but I have just enough to coat my eyes in a golden shimmer. By the time my eyes are lined, and my lashes are lifted with my favorite mascara, I call Marlow out of bed.

"Do you want to go to work or stay home, Mr. Grumpy Pants?" I ask him once he comes back to the door after relieving himself outside. He grunts at me and gallops back to the couch before curling himself into a tight ball.

Alright, I guess that answers that.

I rarely drive anymore, with everything in town being within a five-minute walk, but today's rain has me climbing into the driver's seat of my car. It takes longer than it should, but I hate driving in the rain; I was in a bad accident when I was younger that causes my nerves to get the best of me. My knuckles are white by the time I pull into the shelter parking lot, my fingers wrapped around the wheel in a death grip. I take a moment to calm my breaths and gather my things before turning off the car. I rush inside, sprinting through the rain, only to find Ryker sitting in my office.

"Hey, beautiful." His smile is so beautiful it takes a moment for my mind to catch up to what's happening. Before I can speak, he's on his feet with his arms wrapped around my middle, "what's wrong?"

"Hey, Ry." I hold him tight against me, my face buried into his chest. "It's not fair that you can tell something is wrong just by looking at me. But I'm fine, really. I'll be ok."

"Fallon," his tone is serious and gravely. A rush of heat floods my center from the way he says my name.

"I don't like driving in the rain. It's fine. I don't have far to drive. I'll be ok." I pull away from him to get to my desk as I try to run away from the conversation. I see a cup from The Caffeinated Pumpkin on my desk and pick it up. Lifting the cup to my lips, I take a sip of the sweetest drink to ever be made. That first gulp of coffee just hits different and I let out a soft moan as soon as it touches my taste buds.

Ryker is on me in an instant, spinning me to face him and pressing my body against his. He pries the cup from my hand and places it on the counter next to us just before he devours my mouth. This time feels even more intense as his tongue slips between my lips. It's a sensual dance between us as we find a pace that has both of us moaning, our bodies completely in tune with one another. A soft knock on the door startles us apart.

"God damnit." I'm the one who groans this time and Ryker chuckles. "What?" I call to whoever is at the door.

"Sorry, Fallon. We had a call off because of the rain and we need some help with adoptions." Jade's sweet response sounds from the door.

"I'll be out in five minutes." I call back, hoping she doesn't notice the irritation in my voice hidden beneath the sweet tone.

"I'm glad I'm not the only one affected by the interruptions." He laughs again and presses his lips against mine for a quick kiss. "I'll pick you up after work."

"Ry," I sigh, "I can make it home on my own."

"It's not a question of if you can. It's a matter of why should you have to when you have me, and I can't bear to see you stressed." He pulls me back into his arms. "By the way, I have some news for you if you think you have time."

"What is it?" I ask hesitantly.

"Momma still runs the pumpkin festival more so than me, she likes to keep busy as much as she can," he explains. "I talked to her about including an adoption event and she's all in." His eyes are beaming with pride.

Chapter Eighteen

The memory of Fallon wrapping those thick thighs around my waist whirls through my mind. Beautiful, creamy skin encircled me when I told her about the farm hosting an adoption event at this year's pumpkin festival. The most incredible and joyful smile on her lips had my heart ready to fly through my chest. I nearly exploded in my jeans when she brushed her lips over my face; across my forehead, the bridge of my nose, layering them on each cheekbone until there wasn't a spot left that hadn't received a kiss.

"Damn, Darlin'," I groaned, my hard length pressing against the inside of my jeans. "All that just to say thank you? Hell, I'll do whatever you want if it gets me more of that."

Her answering giggle made my cock swell.

I subtly adjust myself as I climb out of my truck and close the door behind me. It may be raining like the devil, but I've got enough to do to keep me busy before the day is over. The barn doors are open when I walk up, and Jake is there with his head under the hood of the tractor.

"Hey," I call out to him.

"Did you get your fix?" He's just busting my balls, so I flip him off and we both laugh as I go to the other end of the barn. I use this time to clean and organize equipment in the barn. It's been a while since our last big rain, so there's plenty to do.

I'm grateful for Jake's help today, considering how much that tractor is the bane of my existence. Little things have been going wrong with it here and there over the past few years and I'm damn near ready to just throw in the towel and buy a new one. Unfortunately, any time I bring it up, Jake gets offended, saying he can fix it. I don't get it, but better him than me.

It's only ten when I finish in the barn, and I look at my watch and I groan. My least favorite part of what I need to do on rainy days is paperwork. Momma used to take care of all of this, but now she leaves it to me. I bid farewell to Jake for the morning and sprint back to the house, my attempt to outrun the rain completely useless, since I'm soaked through before I'm even halfway to the door. Once I change and dry off, I spend the next few hours hunched over my kitchen table with paperwork and invoices. Everything looks good, thankfully. A few years ago, we had a bit of a scare; the crops weren't where we needed them to be, and we lost a few of the larger stores that bought from us that season.

When the paperwork is finally finished, I glance at my watch only to realize it's already after noon. I stand and stretch my back out before grabbing my phone from the table. My fingers fly across the screen as I send a text to my girl, asking a question I have a feeling I already know the answer to.

It's fascinating to me, I've barely been able to steal moments with her, but I can't get her out of my head. Momma and Elle act like I haven't dated since high school which, I guess I haven't dated *seriously*. I've gone out and casually dated, but nothing has lasted more than a few weeks or a night of hot sweaty fun. What can I say? The women in this town just don't do it for me. Ok, that's a lie; one woman does it for me. Before Fallon moved here, I even tried online dating. That's a hard no for me. *Yikes.*

I stroll out to the porch and pause when I see Jake approaching the house, a goofy smile on his face. I shake my head with a laugh, I know what he's about to say.

"It's good as new!" The grin on his face is infectious and I can't help but return it.

"Thanks, man. I'm going to get lunch for Fallon and me. Do you need anything while I'm out?" I reply with a matching smile.

"Nah, I'm going to head home, I'm wiped out." He gives me one last smile as he waves and approaches his Jeep.

I take the steps down from the porch and walk to my truck. Once inside, I slide the key into the ignition and start the engine. It roars to life; the windshield wipers barely clear the glass enough for me to see a foot in front of me. This is going to be a fun drive. *That's sarcasm in case you didn't pick up on that, by the way.*

It takes me an extra ten minutes than normal to get to the diner, since the roads are nearly flooded. Yea, there's no way in hell Fallon would be able to drive home in this. I park in the closest spot to the door I can find and rush inside. The food is ready, so once I pay, I haul ass back to my truck and cover the final bit of distance to the shelter probably faster than I should. I'm on edge with a frustrating need to see her.

A minute after parking, I'm inside the building, walking quickly into Fallon's office. She's on the floor with her arm draped over reddish fur. I smirk at the sight; she's spooning a dog. I clear my throat.

"Should I be jealous, Darlin'?" I chuckle as she jumps at the sound of my voice .

"Don't do that!" She scolds me, her serious tone telling me I've read the situation wrong. "She's got kennel cough and we're already getting full again. I worry she's going to be put down," her voice cracks.

"I'm sorry, beautiful. What can I do?" I close the distance between us and pull her to her feet. I wrap myself around her, my fingers dipping under the hem of her shirt as I trace small circles on the sensitive skin on her sides. She melts into me, at a loss for words, if even only for a moment.

"Not much we can do unless we can find her a home." She admits into my chest.

We stand there, holding one another for several moments before she pulls away and sits down to eat lunch. She's constantly checking on the dog after every bite or two. I keep my eyes locked on her. Even though she's having a conversation with me, her attention is divided.

"Why don't you adopt her?" I ask with a chuckle.

"I was thinking about fostering her, actually." She admits. "I just worry about more time being dedicated to her and Marlow and not enough –" she stops speaking suddenly.

"Not enough what?" I ask with genuine curiosity. Her face is bright red, telling me she's afraid to say it out loud, whatever it is.

"Nothing, it's nothing." She stutters, "how's your day going?"

"Darlin'," my eyes fixed on her, I arch a brow.

"It's just that," she sighs as she tries to formulate the words. "I don't want to make assumptions about us."

She glares at me, obviously annoyed I'm making her share her thoughts which only endears her to me more.

"...but," I prompt.

"I don't want to take away any time that we could have because I'd have two dogs." She lowers her eyes, no longer able to meet mine.

"Fallon," I call her name. "If you haven't noticed, I very much love animals. The only reason I don't have any pets, apart from Mr. Feeny, which I will blame on Elle for the rest of her life..."

There's a pregnant pause before I continue.

"I lost my black lab, Little Bit," the admission hits me harder than I expected. "He was my best friend, and I just haven't had the heart to adopt another one. I love that you are so invested and have Marlow so involved in your day-to-day life. If anything, I will just find more animal friendly things for us to do." I smile at her.

Fallon's mouth pops open, then closed and then open once more before she finally speaks again.

"You're kind of the real-life embodiment of Prince Charming." She declares with a stray tear falling down her face.

I speak with Tim, my night manager before I leave for the day. I needed to make sure that if another dog gets surrendered tonight, that I will be called. That way I can bring Marlow with me back to the shelter to pick up the sick dog from earlier. She is a reddish deer looking dog that looks like a mix between a Lab and a Pharaoh hound. Otherwise, I will bring him with me tomorrow and we will decide if fostering is a good option for now. Her owners named her Iggy Pup, and she came in with her brother Reggie, but he has already been placed with a foster. I can't find it in my heart to let her go. It breaks my heart to see her sad eyes as I place her back in the kennel before I walk out with Ryker.

His fingers are interlaced with mine as we walk quickly to the truck. It's just drizzling now, but he's refused to let me drive myself home. The need he has to care for me is unlike anything I've experienced in previous relationships. As soon as we're at his truck he turns to me, his fingers are wrapped around the handle but before he opens the door, he presses me into the side of the vehicle, his body flush with mine. Droplets of water soak our skin and clothes, but he doesn't budge to let me in. His face lowers to mine until his breath dances over my lips. I whimper at the closeness, so needy for more.

"How would you feel about picking up Marlow and staying the night with me again?" His voice is deep and husky, the low timbre going straight to my core.

I stand on my tip toes, closing the distance, unable to handle the lack of connection between our mouths. The kiss is sweet but far too short before he chuckles darkly and pulls away from me. *Bastard.*

"I want to feel you next to me when I sleep again. We don't have to do anything more than that until you're ready, Darlin'." His declaration, as pleasant as it is, just adds to my feelings for him.

How am I so far gone for this man already? This isn't normal, is it? I groan inwardly, knowing I'm totally screwed.

"That sounds really nice, actually." I admit shyly. I can feel my cheeks heat under his blue eyes.

He releases me, and I giggle at how drenched we both are as we enter the truck. He got me wet, in more ways than one, but I'm not quite sure I'm ready to disclose that to him just yet. He places a hand on my thigh and squeezes the slick skin as he shifts the truck into drive and takes me home to get Marlow.

Ryker goes into Elle's apartment to talk to her while I run upstairs. I toss together a quick overnight bag, throwing in pajamas, clothes for tomorrow, my bathroom stuff, and Marlow's necessities. *If this is going to become a normal thing, me staying here and especially if I adopt a second dog, I am going to need to double up on dog food bags.* No, I can't think about that yet. This is only the second time I'm staying over. Don't be crazy.

I climb the stairs to Ryker's room with Marlow close on my heels. We just finished dinner and it's only seven, but since he works so early, I didn't want to keep him up too late. I'm pulling on a pair of sleep shorts when he walks in, a low growl rumbling from his chest as he strips off his shirt. He tosses it at me, the cotton hitting me in the chest as my mouth dries at the sight.

The man has a two, four, no, *six* pack and that deep V at the waist that I want to trail with my tongue. *I did not just think that. Yes, yes, I did. Crap.* His chest looks broad under his shirts but seeing him bare is an entirely different experience. God damn. He has a long scar high up on his ribs, just under his pecs. I need to know what caused it. I lift the shirt that he just threw at me and glance down at it before looking back at him, still mesmerized by the sight before me.

"What's this for?" I ask.

"I loved seeing you sleep in my shirt the other night." He admits nonchalantly as he kicks off his boots and sets them by the door.

"Ok..." I keep my eyes on him as I raise my tank top over my head so that I'm standing before him in just a light pink lace bra and my sleep shorts. I know I'm being a tease, but he kind of walked into this. I slowly drag the shirt over my head, making a show of sliding my arms through the sleeves while not dropping eye contact.

"Fuck me," he groans as he shucks his jeans off and throws them in a hamper. I gasp sharply in surprise at how hard and thick he is.

Oh, baby. If you only knew how much self-control, it's taking me not to just hop on and ride you so hard we break your bed.

Nope. Nope. Not gonna say it out loud. No way!

I climb into bed, and Marlow flops down on the floor next to me. Ryker raises a brow and walks over to where I lay down. He climbs over Marlow and hovers over me, his lips pressing soft kisses to my lips, before he sits back on his knees and lifts me with ease into his arms before placing me on the other side of the bed.

"Darlin', I will always take the side closest to the door. Elle scared me shitless when she got into true crime podcasts and then that damn Schitts' Creek episode." He chuckles, "I'll take on any murderers before they can get to you."

And just like that, I realize I'm absolutely smitten with this man.

Ryker scoots under the blankets and turns the bedroom light off as I grab my E-reader. He may need to sleep, but I can catch up on some reading and still be with him. His arms fold around me and he pulls me into his chest. He presses a soft kiss to the back of my neck. We don't need to speak, just the feel of his body against mine, the warmth of his skin pressed to my back, is enough. His breathing steadies quickly as I am reading, before I know it he's fast asleep and I'm lost back in the world of Solis Lake Academy.

Chapter Twenty

Only an hour after I've fallen asleep, I feel her squirming against me. My eyes flutter open, and I can see she's still got her E-reader in hand. I do my best not to move so she doesn't realize I'm awake. Her chest heaves as she takes deep breaths. Something has her turned on; I can smell her arousal. My dick hardens as soon as I realize just how turned on she is. Fuck, she smells good.

I glance inconspicuously over her shoulder at the screen of the E-reader and see a flurry of words, but my eyes are still sleepy, I hone in on a few words though: cock, thrust, cum. Oh, my girl is reading a dirty book.

My fingers twitch where they lay over the waistband of her shorts. Her breathing doesn't change, so she must not notice. I sneak my fingertips under the waistband to find she has no panties on. She's seriously going to be the death of me. I trail my hand down her shorts even further; she's so invested in her smut that she hasn't noticed I'm not asleep. It's not until my fingertips graze her clit that her body goes still.

"Ryker," she whispers into the dark room.

"Mmm," I respond as I nip the sensitive skin behind her ear.

I swipe the pads of my fingers along her folds before dipping in and exploring her arousal. Her shorts are soaked through. I chuckle darkly as her breathing becomes ragged. Adjusting my wrist, I find her entrance, pulling a moan from deep in her throat as she grips my forearm, trying to hold me still.

"Darlin', let me help. I just want to feel you." My voice is gravelly in her ear from the little bit of sleep I've had. "I don't need anything other than to hear you call out my name when I make you strangle my fingers."

"Ohmygod," it comes out as one word as she melts back into me. Her E-reader forgotten as it falls onto the bed next to her.

She gives me access to her most sensitive spot, spreading her legs. I hook one over my hip and explore her. My lips are on her again, pressing light kisses against the column of her throat. My fingers dive inside her, sliding deeper as she relaxes. She's panting as I find that spot deep inside her that has her crying out my name. Fallon bucks her hips when my thumb finds her clit, my other fingers pumping in and out, massaging her inner walls.

"Ry!" Her body trembles as her cunt tightens around my fingers, the release ripping through her like a tidal wave. "Yes, Ryker!"

I don't stop moving, my fingers still wringing the pleasure from her body until she finally relaxes against me. My cock is throbbing, and I nearly burst in my briefs as she comes down from her orgasm, soft whimpers and moans escape her lips before she parts her thighs and releases my hand. I chuckle and lift my fingers to my mouth, sucking them into my mouth to lick them clean.

"God damn, Darlin', you taste like heaven." I praise. She giggles and wriggles her body against me trying to get closer. I groan at the sensation. "Fallon, I can only hold back for so long. You're playing with fire right now, beautiful."

"Mmm..." is the only sound that slips from her lips before I hear her breathing steady as she falls asleep, satiated in my arms.

The soft beeping of my phone alarm gradually pulls me from sleep. Fallon is still asleep, but laying half on top of me. It seems I rolled onto my back during the night, and she wasn't close enough. I chuckle to myself. *My little spider monkey.* I press my lips to her forehead before I slip out from underneath her and head into the bathroom to wash up before I start my day.

Quietly walking down the stairs and the short hallway to my kitchen, I find Jake with coffee in hand. He furrows his brow as he hands me a mug and I cock one back in a silent question.

"Why the hell do you look like you haven't slept?" He blurts out the question so damn loud I slap a hand over his mouth.

"Fallon is upstairs sleeping, jackass." I groan just as I hear nails clicking across the upstairs floor. Shit she's up. Turning to look down the hallway I just came through, I see Marlow standing there with his head cocked like he wants in on the conversation as well. "Do you need to go out, bud?" I chuckle as the big fluff ball races toward me.

Jake, being closest to the door, pushes it open just wide enough for Marlow to sneak out. We watch him through the door as he does his business and runs back to the porch, whining to be let back in. Jake barely gets the door open before the dog races past us and rushes back up to my room. *I feel ya, I would love nothing more than to crawl back in bed with her too.*

"Sooooooo," Jake taunts like a teenage girl trying to get gossip.

"Nope, get out, let's get to work. I'm going to have to come back and take her to work in a couple of hours." I do my best to sidestep the interrogation.

He stands there sipping his coffee quietly, his eyes locked on me. I roll mine at him, waiting for the bastard to say whatever is on his mind. A smirk dances on his lips before he finally lets it out.

"You look happy," the smirk turns into a full-on grin. "Really happy. In fact, I don't think I've ever seen you like this before, even in all the time I've known you."

"I don't know how I should take that." I choke as my coffee goes down the wrong pipe. *Shit.*

He shakes his head and just walks off. In truth, I am happy. The last serious, or even semi-serious relationship I had was in high school and that was nothing compared to this. Lexi was a good girl but that's all she was, a girl. Even if she hadn't moved away, I know we wouldn't have made it much further than high school. I wasn't in love with her. Not like... Whoa, holy shit. Am I...? Jesus Christ.

I'm in love with Fallon. The thought slams into me, the air rushing from my lungs in an audible whoosh. The image of the most beautiful woman I've ever seen, fast asleep in my bed upstairs drifts into my mind. She's exactly where she should be: with me. Now, I just have to pray she might love me, too.

Chapter Twenty-One

My eyelids are still heavy, not ready to open when I feel the mattress dip. I groan and try to pull the sheet over my face to hide the rude stream of sunlight. The sheet is stuck on something heavy. I moan, this time feeling too tired to fight it, I throw my arm over my face. Ryker's T-shirt rides up, exposing my stomach, cellulite and all. A low throaty chuckle startles me, and I freeze, then slowly lower my arm. Suddenly, very self conscious, I pull the shirt down quickly to cover my body. My eyes slowly open to find a beautiful man sitting next to me with his gaze glued to me. The expression on his face tells me exactly what he's thinking. Oh my god, it wasn't a dream. Suddenly I feel *very* naked in front of him.

"Good morning, beautiful. How did you sleep?" His smooth voice relaxes me in an unfair manner, my anxieties melting away.

I stretch in my spot on the bed and smile at him, "morning handsome. I could use a little more." I admit and then shoot up realizing I have to be at work. "Wait, what time is it?"

"It's only seven, you don't have to be in for another hour." He chuckles. "I just got back inside and turned your alarm off so I could wake you."

My body relaxes and I collapse back onto the mattress. "You scared the hell out of me. I thought I was late."

"Sorry, gorgeous. You will be, though, if you don't start moving." He chuckles as he leans down and presses his lips to mine. My hands find his hair and my fingers grab hold, deepening the kiss. Morning breath be damned. He groans into my mouth and lifts me into his arms as he devours me with a fiery passion that has heat pooling between my thighs. His chest is pressed so hard against mine I can feel his muscles flex, only making me want more. I whimper when he abruptly ends the kiss, pressing his forehead to mine.

"Good morning," I giggle the greeting again this time through ragged breaths.

"You enjoy torturing me, don't you?" He groans.

"I wouldn't say that," I smirk. "I would like to thank you for last night, though." My cheeks flush as soon as the words leave my mouth.

"Stay over again?" He asks with a wicked grin.

"I would love to, but I'm going to adopt her, so she'll be with me." Visions of the sweet red deer dog flash through my mind.

"I told you, Darlin'," he sits back up and pulls me with him as he points to himself with a thumb. "Animal person. Bring Marlow and – wait, what are you going to name her?"

"Haley Bob," the name pops out with ease. "I re-watched One Tree Hill recently. She's my favorite character," I explain.

Ryker's smile widens as he takes me in. This man is so beyond my wildest dreams. I giggle when he slaps my thigh prompting me to stand up and get ready for the day.

After daydreaming in the shower for longer than I should have, I'm now officially running late. I rush down the stairs with Marlow on my heels to find Ryker waiting for us. He is sitting at the kitchen table with a steaming mug of coffee. Now that my mind isn't hazy with sleep; I take in his tight jeans and white T-shirt. He wears the same thing nearly every day, but damn, does he wear it well. He grins and offers me a sip, which I gladly accept. Still no flavor. Ugh.

"If I'm going to be waking up here, I'm going to have to stop by the store and grab some creamer and sugar at the very least." I swallow down the bitter liquid.

Don't get me wrong, I love coffee. It smells like heaven, and it allows me to function as a normal human being. However, without the extras of flavors and creamer it tastes like an ashtray. I said what I said.

"Do you like any flavors besides your precious pumpkin spice?" Ryker teases me.

"Sure, but sugar and creamer are fine for the first jolt of the day," I cuddle into his side.

"I'll stop by the store on the way back." He declares in a tone that tells me it's not up for negotiation. He wants me to bring not one, but two dogs to his house tonight, and he's supplying my bougie coffee addiction? Is this heaven?

Marlow and Haley Bob are both snuggled up on Marlow's bed in my office. The moment I introduced them it was game over. They've been attached at the hip since, and it's been goddamn adorable. Part of me wonders if he'll be more comfortable staying at home now during the day since he won't be alone. I quickly scratch that thought; they're both coming with me.

I'm on the phone with a representative of New Life Animal Rescue who has requested to take a few of our long-term dogs. They've called in again to let me know they've arranged transport for tomorrow. The woman on the phone is so kind; she's been running the rescue for a number of years now, and makes it a point to take from as many shelters as she can.

A couple of hours later, I've finished getting things ready for the transfer and my head is pounding. I glance up when I hear a knock on the door to see Elle standing there with a bag from the diner in her hand.

"You are an angel." I smile widely, realizing the pounding in my head is from a lack of food.

"Bestie, how the hell did you survive before me?" She laughs.

"Honestly, I have no clue." She leans over the desk and gives me an awkward hug.

"Who in the world is this cutie?" She gasps when she realizes Marlow isn't the only dog laying on his bed.

"Oh, uhm, so...how do you feel about a tenant having two dogs?" I chuckle nervously, realizing I should have run this by her.

"Are you kidding me!" She squeals, clapping her hands in excitement just like Mrs. Addams did the other day.

"No…" I bite my lip, anxious for her to give me a yes or no. "This is Haley Bob." I announce.

"Aren't you the sweetest little girl to have ever graced our presence!" Elle's baby talk gives me my answer, and I breathe a sigh of relief.

"Ok, good. I'm glad that's out of the way," I snort as I open the bag of food, pulling out a burger and fries. We take the time to catch up, and I bring her up to speed on the previous night's activities. We're all adults and she asked, so I told her about the relief he gave while I was reading. I probably won't give her the specifics she asks about regarding other things. Although just from what I've felt through our clothes, I'd have plenty to discuss.

Chapter Twenty-Two

My goal to have dinner ready for her before she gets back is running closer than I'd like. The steak I have on the grill is just about ready to serve, but the vegetable medley I prepared is being difficult – because inanimate objects such as food can be difficult – and taking its sweet old time. Mr. Feeny is laying on the bench next to me while I stare out at the horizon. The sky has that beautiful pinkish orangey color that reminds me of a summer peach. I take a long pull of my beer while music plays through the outdoor speakers, smiling as I listen to the lyrics. I glance at my phone only to realize Fallon should be here by now. As if she's read my mind, I hear gravel crunching under tires. I look up at the same time as Mr. Feeny who stretches out as soon as I stand.

I hear her mutter something to the dogs as she lets Marlow and her newest addition, Haley Bob, out of her car. Marlow leads Haley to me, and I pet them both. They both greet Mr. Feeny with a quick sniff from all parties. Thankfully, there are no issues between any of them. Alright, alright, alright – when did Matthew McConaughey get here? Maybe *he* is my fox.

Fallon is at my side a moment later and I wrap her in an embrace, the music is still playing as we start to sway back and forth. My hands snake down her back to cup her deliciously full ass. The shorts she's wearing today are shorter than what she's worn before. My long fingers touch the back of her bare thighs when I reach for her ass. She giggles when I dip and pull her back up to sway with me again. The tank top she has on does nothing to contain her large perky tits, and I take full advantage of the view. I grin when her eyes meet mine and I start to hum along with the Brett Young song currently playing.

"Life's a dance and I want to dance with you."

She gasps when she realizes what I said but before she responds, I press my lips to hers. A need to possess her, to claim her, takes over. My tongue swipes inside her mouth to taste her again. In my mind, I know it's not even been a day, but my heart, my body, say it's been an eternity.

"Ry," she whimpers as she pulls away.

"Darlin'," I reply with my forehead pressed to hers, not quite ready to let go of her yet.

"I – I missed you today," she says shyly. I feel the words she wants to say.

"I missed you, too." The corners of my lips twitch as they pull into a smirk.

We let the music continue through the outdoor speakers as we sit down and have dinner. The sun slowly sets, the colorful sky turning into a dark blue and finally an inky black as we talk about everything. From our day during the hours we were apart to our hopes for the future. She confesses she'd like to run her own rescue one day. I tell her I'd like to buy more land to expand the farm and hire more help. There are so many crops we could grow outside of just pumpkins.

I've never told anyone that, not even my parents. I'm not sure how they'd respond to my desire to change our family's legacy. This farm has been in the Addams family for generations. A loud yawn escapes me, and Fallon chuckles, checking the time.

"Come on, let's get to bed." She holds out her hand for me to take. We both say goodnight to Mr. Feeny and give scritches in his favorite spot before we lead the dogs inside for the night.

Haley and Marlow follow behind us as we walk into the house. I spin Fallon around to face me as soon as we cross the threshold, and she shrieks at the sudden movement. The dogs jump at the sudden noise and run off through the house. A low chuckle erupts from my chest as I lean in and press another soft kiss to her lips. This time, I don't take it further. I'm stalling, I know I am. I may have bought something for Marlow and Haley. Now I'm panicked that it's going to be too much, too fast and scare her away.

Don't fuck this up, Ryker.

With a sweet smile, she turns back to the hall and walks up the stairs. Her creamy thighs on full display as she walks ahead of me. I rush to catch up, smacking her ass as she reaches the final step.

"Now who's torturing who, hmm?" She teases as we continue to my room.

As soon as she enters, I hear a loud gasp. She pokes her head back out into the hall as I cautiously approach. There are unshed tears brimming in her eyes as she looks at me. *Shit, I fucked up. God dammit.*

"If it's too much or too fast I can return –" She doesn't allow me to finish before she's climbing me like a tree. Her legs are wrapped around my waist, her lips on mine. She peppers kisses over every inch of skin on my face before she fumbles to tear my shirt off over my head. I let her down easily and sit on the edge of the bed. I'm startled, unsure how to respond. Did I not fuck up? Her hands trail down along the ridges of my abs.

"Fallon," I groan.

She doesn't stop, she spends the next few minutes exploring every last fucking inch of bare skin before she undoes the button and zipper of my pants. I keep my eyes trained on her. I watch as she hooks her thumbs into the waistband of my jeans and tugs, an unspoken request for me to lift my hips so she can pull them down. I oblige, I'd be a damn fool not to.

I'm thankful to have gone commando because the appreciative, needy whine that leaves her lips when my cock bursts free is the sexiest thing I've ever heard.

"Ry," she breathes, her eyes wide as she takes in my generous size.

Chapter Twenty-Three

I'm not an innocent girl; I've had sex, been in relationships. Only two one-night-stands though – zero out of ten, do not recommend. Especially when you wear your heart on your sleeve like me. The point is, this isn't the first dick I've seen. But God damn, is it the best I've ever laid eyes on.

My mouth is watering as soon as it springs from his jeans. Jesus, Mary, Joseph and the camel, it's magnificent. I lower myself to my knees in front of him where he sits on the edge of the bed. My tongue darts out to moisten my lips and I hear a low rumble from his chest. He needs me as much as I need to taste him. His heated gaze is on me as I lean forward with a smirk on my face and lower my mouth to his beautiful dick. I swipe my tongue across the shining tip, the salty taste of his pre-cum dancing across my taste buds. A tortured moan leaves both of us at once.

"Darlin'," he rasps at the contact.

My tongue swirls around the crown of his dick and his head drops back between his shoulders. I slide him in deeper and hollow my cheeks. Every part of me needs to make him feel as good as he made me feel last night. I fuck him with my mouth, taking him to the back of my throat. Ryker's moans fill the room, turning me on even more and making me want to take him over the edge. I hum around his length as I swallow around the tip. A low curse leaves his mouth as he digs his nails into my scalp and grips my hair as he takes what he needs. My eyes water as he thrusts into my throat with no care in the world but his own pleasure. It makes me feel better than it should to be used by this man like this.

"Fuck, Fallon. Darlin', Jesus – FUCK!" He growls as his cock thickens even more in my mouth before exploding down my throat.

My nails bite into the flesh of his hips as I hold him in my mouth to make sure I get every last drop of his salty release before swallowing all that he gave me. As soon as I'm sure he's spent, I pull back and sit on my heels. A shy smile plays on my lips when he lifts me into his arms. He's holding me between his muscular thighs as his lips connect to mine for a sweet gentle kiss.

"Thank you," I say before he even has a chance to catch his breath.

"You're thanking me?" He asks, dumbfounded. "Darlin', that's not..."

I giggle and swat his chest. "I'm not thanking you for that, though I'm happy to provide a repeat performance any time," I wink at him. "No. Thank you for this," I wave to where there is a large dog bed at the foot of his bed for Marlow and Haley.

When I say bed, I mean it's got a frame and looks like a daybed, but for dogs.

"I just wanted you to know I mean it when I say they're both welcome here." Ryker looks at me with an unsure smile. "I was worried I went too fast with getting that." He admits, his body tense. The way his eyes penetrate into me even though I stare at him with a blank expression has me screaming internally. I don't want to do this, to have this conversation after what just transpired between us.

"I know we haven't talked about it, but Elle's hinted that your last relationship ended badly." His voice is low, "I didn't want to push you too fast."

I sigh knowing I can't fully move on unless I share this. So, I do. I climb onto the bed next to Ryker and spill my heart out to him. I tell him about finding Kyle and Ruth in our new bed, finding out they had been messing around behind my back for months. His body is stiff next to me as I speak. When I drop the final bomb on him, that just before I gave my notice at my old job, they had sent me an announcement of their pending nuptials and a baby due in a few months. An actual paper announcement, they took the time to hand write the envelopes and everything.

"It was a final slap in the face. I don't know why they did it. They got their happily ever after. Them deciding to shove it in my face like that nearly gutted me all over again." I laugh but there's no humor behind it, "It just solidified that coming here was the right decision."

When I'm finally done sharing the worst memories of my life, I glance up to see Ryker's eyes. They're full of pain, anger, but also something softer. I shrug my shoulders, unable to express anymore emotions. My eyes are filled with tears, but I refuse to shed a single one over the people that nearly destroyed me. Sometimes the memories just hurt so badly they try to make their way out.

"Selfishly, I'm glad he fucked up so royally because it brought you to me." He admits, as he pulls me close to him, his voice is harsh, "I'm sorry that you've had to deal with such a shitty loss, not just a partner but a friend. That –" he sighs, "that can sometimes be even harder."

I nod and clear my throat. "I don't want to let this damper our night anymore."

He pulls me on top of him so that I'm straddling his legs, my thick thighs on either side of him. I gasp as a laugh escapes. He crushes me against his chest, his muscular arms holding me tight. Our lips collide again, and he refuses to let me go, even when I complain that I'm going to hurt him if we stay in this position for too long. He growls into my lips and holds me even tighter. At some point we end up laying down on the bed, our limbs tangled together. After making out like a couple of teenagers for I'm not sure how long, he lets out a yawn.

"Aw, are you turning into a pumpkin?" I giggle when I see just how tired he is.

"What?" He asks, not understanding the reference.

"I know you were an only child, but Elle had to have made you watch Disney movies," not hiding my disbelief. "Hell in the time I've known her she's made me watch Disney movies I didn't even know existed."

There's no response, I glance over at the man who is still wrapped around me, his chest heaves with steady breaths as he sleeps peacefully.

Chapter Twenty-Four

Fallon has been staying with me most nights over the last couple of weeks. Even if she hasn't wanted to take it all the way, I've been content with having her in my arms while I sleep. Don't get me wrong, there've been many nights I've woken up to her being hot and bothered by whatever the book of the day is, because that's how fast this woman reads – that I will get her off. She's just not quite ready for more from me. She's scared, and after finding out what her shithead of an ex did, I can't blame her.

I walk into my room after finishing what I needed to do around the patches today to find her still sound asleep. Marlow is on the bed next to her, but I don't see Haley anywhere at first. Then her foot twitches from where it's poking out under the covers, I chuckle quietly to myself. That dog is adorable, but so damn bizarre.

I cross to the connected bathroom and turn on the shower. After washing up quickly I climb out and dry off, tossing on a new pair of briefs. I've got something planned for her this afternoon. I climb back into bed and nuzzle against the column of her throat. She begins to stir so I give her a gentle kiss.

"Good morning, Darlin'," I grin against her lips.

Fallon groans and throws a pillow over her face, making me chuckle. I press my lips to her throat, tossing the blanket from her body as I pepper kisses down her throat. The T-shirt I gave her to wear last night has ridden up so much it's exposing the silky skin just under her breasts. I arch a brow at her from my position, a silent question since she hasn't moved or tried to push me away. My lips softly brush against her skin and her breath catches. Swiping my tongue against her flesh, Fallon arches into me instead of covering herself. My mouth twists into a wicked smile as I slowly slide up her shirt to expose her bare breasts. Fuck they're gorgeous. I've seen her before; she's gotten changed in front of me plenty of times. But God damn, every single time I see them it makes my cock weep.

I swirl my tongue around her nipple and bite softly, Fallon's moan fills the room. I move over to the other and bite down before sucking the pebbled peak into my mouth. She gasps, which for whatever reason makes both dogs lose their minds and headbutt me in the shoulder until I am no longer hovering over her.

"Oh my god." Her giggle is contagious as she sits up and pulls the shirt down over herself.

I grumble and adjust myself as she moves to sit on her heels in front of me.

"I'm sorry, Ry." She giggles again.

"You're going to be the death of me, woman." I groan and lift her in one swift motion to her feet. She squeals but doesn't fight me. "Get moving, we have somewhere to be, beautiful."

Her laughter fills the room as she hops off the bed and heads to the bathroom to shower.

Two hours later, we're parked at Galena Cellars Winery and Vineyard. It's only an hour from Hollow Heights, and according to some online research, they allow dogs. She glances at me from her seat in my truck and looks back at the dogs.

"Yes, I checked. It's why we're here." I answer her unspoken question as I slide out of the truck and let Marlow and Haley Bob out, securing each of their leashes. They walk plastered side by side, as though they're worried about losing each other. We make our way to the other side where Fallon is standing, waiting for us.

Her earlier confusion has transformed into the most beautiful smile. I take her hand in mine as we walk toward the tasting deck. My heart swells in my chest when we sit down at the table, both dogs are at our feet and a live band is playing somewhere nearby. The sun is beating down behind her, and the way the rays illuminate the space around her has Fallon looking like the most beautiful woman on the planet. I pull out my phone and snap a picture while she's not paying attention, grinning at the serene look on her face.

"This is incredible," she praises.

"I thought you'd like it. Wine *and* we can bring the dogs," I respond playfully.

Just then a server comes over to the table to take our order. My girl orders a wine flight while I get a local IPA. It only takes a few minutes before our drinks arrive, each of us taking a sip.

"Ry?" She calls while I'm leaning down petting Haley. The way that nickname sounds on her lips makes my dick throb in my jeans.

"Yes, Darlin'?" I respond, as I sit back up and give her my full attention.

"Thank you, I know you're dealing with so much and taking things slower than I'm sure you'd like." She starts, her eyes glistening with unshed tears. "This just means the world to me that you would find a place like this. That you make sure to include them in everything. I know – I know it may seem silly that it makes me this emotional, but thank you for caring this much."

I stare at her for a few moments, my mind trying to formulate the words to express just how serious I am about everything concerning her. The only way is to just lay it all out there I suppose. I take a deep breath before I speak.

"Fallon, I would wait until the end of time for you. Your past may not have shown you your worth. But Darlin', I will spend every single day for the rest of my life showing you just how incredible you are." My smile is soft as I continue. "I fall more and more in love with you every day."

It takes a moment, but her eyes go wide as saucers when the words sink in.

Chapter Twenty-Five

"**I**'m sorry, you – you what?" I blurt out the question as I choke down a sob.

"You heard me, Darlin', I love you." The wickedly handsome grin on his stupid face makes my heart explode. He stands to his feet and rounds the table to get to me.

"You – me – we barely know each other!" I'm stammering, my breaths coming quicker and quicker as I replay his words. Everything about this is wrong, why am I freaking out when I feel the same way. How does he feel this way when it hasn't been long enough?

"And yet," he shrugs as he holds his hand out to me, "care to dance, beautiful?"

"Wait." My hands reach for his and I stand following him. Yes, I know I said to wait but my feet and brain aren't working together. Ryker has

Haley and Marlow's leashes as he leads all of us down to the patio where a few other couples are dancing. The dogs somehow follow his instruction to sit and stay in place while he wraps me in his arms.

He sways us to the music like we do most nights that we are at his place when the weather cooperates. Our eyes are locked on one another, I see nothing but adoration, longing, and love. My heart swells as I take a deep breath.

"Ry," I loop my arms around his neck, the stupid smirk is back which just makes my lips break into a smile. "I love you, too."

"I know." He winks and spins us around the patio until the song ends.

A giggle bursts from my lips as a tear slides down my cheek. Ryker presses a soft kiss along the wet streak which just makes even more fall. Damn him and his sweetness.

"Can we go home?" I ask quietly.

My heart is ready to burst through my chest. I've been wanting more of him since the first night he woke and caught me during a smutty scene. Selfishly, I think I've held back because I have been subconsciously punishing Ryker for what Kyle did to me. It's unfair, I know. But after tonight, with what we both confessed? If we had been home, I would have mounted him wherever we were at the time. On the patio, in the house, really it wouldn't have mattered.

I need him. *All* of him.

The drive from the winery seems to be taking longer than the drive there. It doesn't help that no matter what I do, I can't get the ache between my legs to go away. No matter how much I squeeze my thighs together it won't stop the pulsing need. I throw my head back against the headrest in exasperation and I feel Ry's eyes on me.

"Are you ok over there?" He chuckles darkly. It's obvious he knows *exactly* what my problem is by the way he places his hand on my thigh and squeezes so close to my core.

My brain short circuits and I forget how to speak for the last few minutes of the ride. I come to when we're pulling onto the lane to his house. As soon as he parks, I jump out of the truck and let Haley and Marlow out to do their business before we head inside.

Ryker rounds the bed of the truck and cages me against the side.

"You never answered me," his mouth is close to my ear when he speaks. The warm breath caresses my neck which sends a rush of heat to my core. Jesus, when I didn't think it could get any worse.

"I want to go to bed." My voice comes out husky, dripping with desire.

After we round up the dogs and get them both inside, I tell Ryker to give me a few minutes before he comes up. I hear him scooping out dry dog food into their bowls as I rush up the stairs and lock myself in the bathroom.

I strip down to my pink lace bra and panties and look at myself in the mirror. My mind begins to spiral as I think about what's going to happen as soon as I open the door. *Shit. Fuck. Oh god. Am I ready for this?* Before I talk myself out of going through with what I know we both want, I grab my phone from the pocket of my discarded jeans. I tap the screen furiously until I find the contact I need and press call. She picks up on the second ring.

"Hey, Bestie Boo, what's up?" Elle sounds so cheerful. A stark contrast to the panic settling in my chest.

"I'm spiraling," I admit into the phone as quietly as possible while I pace back and forth in the small room.

"Whoa, what's going on?" She asks, her voice changing from cheerful to concerned in a second.

"I think we're going to. I mean I want to. *We* want to." I stutter trying to find the words, "I'm so fucking scared, Elle. What if it all goes to hell?"

"Fallon, if there was even a remote possibility that he was going to hurt you," she speaks softly as she starts over with her thought, "If he was going to use you, you wouldn't be there. I'm not going to let you get hurt. I saw you when you first moved here babe, you were a completely different person. I have also known him since I was a kid, he doesn't take this kind of time or energy with anyone. Plus, I'm pretty sure Momma Addams would beat him if he hurt you or fucked this up. She's more excited about the adoption event at the pumpkin fest than you are."

"Thank you, I love you Elle." I chuckle softly at her response. We say our goodbyes and disconnect before I unlock the door to walk back into the room. When I make my reappearance, I find Ry closing the bedroom door with the dogs on the other side. I can't help but giggle. He spins on his heel when he hears me, his jaw pops open as he takes me in.

"Yea, they're staying out there for now." Ryker smirks, his eyes raking over my body. . "You are fucking perfect."

I flush at his words.

"Thank you," I reply shyly.

The moment Fallon emerges from the bathroom, all my blood rushes south. My dick is going to have an imprint of the zipper along the length.

"Yea, they're staying out there for now." Her curves fill out the cups of the lacy bra so beautifully. My eyes roam down her body, her soft stomach on full display has my mouth watering. When they land on her panties—if they can even be called that, given there's barely anything to them—I adjust myself, fuck being discrete about it. "You are fucking perfect."

Her skin tinges pink as she takes in my words, until the color almost matches the lingerie.

"Thank you," her shy reply only makes my cock weep with need.

"Fuck," I growl and close the distance between us, caging her in against the wall.

The tension is already too high, and I can't wait any longer. I cup her cheeks with my hands and my lips are on hers in an instant. Fallon's soft moans at the connection have me ready to devour her. I swipe my tongue across her lips, needing to taste every part of her tonight. She allows access and it's a mix of teeth and tongue clashing together. There's nothing slow about this kiss compared to others we've shared. It's full of need and lust.

I glide my hands down Fallon's sides, her soft skin pebbling at the warmth of my touch. I drop to my knees before her, glancing up as I lower my mouth to her core. She lets out a breathy moan when she feels my breath on her. I chuckle as I press gentle kisses on the inside of each thigh. She's whining by the time I return to her center. I swipe my tongue up the length of her slit over her panties and suck hard when I reach her clit. A guttural moan escapes her at the sensation. I pull back just enough to give her a little space.

"Ry! Please!" She begs.

"Darlin', I don't care if a twister comes and carries this house off to Oz tonight, I am nowhere near done with you yet." I hook my thumbs into the waistband of her panties and drag them down her lusciously thick thighs. She places her hands on my shoulders so she can step out of them.

Grinning up at her, I lift one thigh and hook it over my shoulder, my arm wrapping around it to hold her in place. My tongue darts out and swipes against her clit. Her soft moans just bring a smile to my face. I lift her other leg to hook over my shoulder and she tries to argue.

"Ry, no! I'm too heavy!"

Instead of responding verbally, I lock both of my arms around her thighs, pressing her into the wall as I bury my face between her legs. My mouth latches on, devouring her pussy as she writhes against me from the overwhelming sensation. I alternate between sucking her clit and lapping at it with my tongue. She sobs, begging for me to make her come. Her nails dig into my scalp as she holds my head still. I flatten my tongue against her pussy, and she rides my face, taking control of her pleasure, until she falls over the edge.

"Ryker! Yes! Oh god! Ryker!" She cries out, the sounds muffled by how her thighs are holding my face hostage. I'm loving every fucking second of it.

It takes a few moments for her to come down, I swipe my tongue against her already sensitive clit, making her buck into my face. She releases me, quickly sliding from my shoulders to stand back on her feet. I chuckle darkly as she pants and holds her hands out in surrender.

"I need a minute."

"Bed, now," I command with a wink. "You can have your minute there."

She hurries over to the bed as she unhooks the pink lace wrapped around her chest and tosses it to the floor before collapsing onto her back. Fuck, she's gorgeous and all fucking mine. I pull the T-shirt over my head and toss it off to the side. My dick is aching for relief after being confined for so long. When I unzip my jeans, I let out a soft sigh. The pressure was starting to become unbearable. I shove the jeans and briefs down and kick them off toward the discarded T-shirt.

I saunter over to the bed where she's since propped herself up on her elbows. She grins when she sees me getting closer. My god this woman is incredible.

"Ry," Fallon's voice is soft when she calls my name and parts her legs for me to see her glistening cunt.

My feet start moving, my body simply drawn to her. I climb onto the bed, kneeling between her parted legs and press my lips to hers, devouring her in another passion-filled kiss. She lets out a needy moan when she tastes herself on my tongue. I growl into the kiss; I need to feel her. I pull away and move to get off the bed. I bought condoms after she stayed over for the first time. Listen – a man can dream.

Pulling the box from the nightstand, I tear it open, grabbing one out. I tear the foil packet with my teeth and make quick work of sheathing my cock. Fallon's eyes are glued to me as I position myself back between her legs. I swipe the tip of my cock up her slit, coating it in her arousal.

"Are you sure, Darlin'?" I ask, praying she hasn't changed her mind. I'd never push her, but good lord, the need to feel this woman has me damn near feral.

"I need you," Fallon whimpers. It's the sweetest damn sound.

Without another word I notch myself at her entrance and slide the head of my cock inside her. Fuck, she's so tense.

"Baby, I need you to relax or I'm never going to fit." She takes a deep breath, her muscles loosening a little bit at a time.

"Oh god!" She moans as I work my way inside her.

When I'm fully seated, I give her a moment to adjust to my size. She's so goddamn tight I don't know how I'm going to last more than a minute. I grind against her, the friction on her clit making her squeeze around me.

"Fallon, I'm holding on by a thread," I choke out, "If you keep that up; I'm going to be done before I start."

She giggles which does nothing to help my self-control. I pull out and thrust back in, making her cry out in pleasure. I grin as I fuck her, slowly pulling out and then sliding in to fill her completely again and again.

"Ry! Oh god, please!" She cries out when I swipe the tip of my thumb over her clit. I know I'm not going to last much longer, and I can't fly over that edge without her.

Chapter Twenty-Seven

Ryker collapses on top of me, calling out my name as he finds his release. I let out a breathy giggle, making him curse. His cock pulses from deep inside me, drawing a moan from my lips. He slowly pulls out and sits up to remove the condom. Once it's tied off, he tosses it in the small trash can next to the bed.

"My god woman," he groans as he lays back down next to me.

"Back at you," I giggle again, too damn blissed out from the orgasm to say much more.

"Fuck, Darlin', every time I hear your giggle now, I'm going to be walking around with a hardon," He smirks at me, "The way your pussy strangled my dick every time you giggled while I was inside you...Jesus fucking Christ."

"Hmm, really now?" I flash a wicked smirk at him.

"Oh hell," he chuckles.

We lay together for a while, his fingers tracing circles on my skin. The feel of his bare skin against mine is intoxicating. Our conversations flow so easily, as always, and I find myself relaxing into him.

I wake wrapped in Rykers embrace, the body heat and blanket draped over me are a cocoon of warmth. With a glance at my phone, I realize he only has twenty minutes left before he needs to wake for the day. I carefully lift his arm and slide out from under him. A wide smile pulls at my lips as I toss on his t-shirt from the night before. Enjoying the smell of him on me even though he's still asleep I open the bedroom door to find Marlow and Haley cuddled up by the door. They both startle and jump up excitedly at my reappearance. I walk past, urging them to follow me down the stairs. As soon as we reach the hall at the bottom of the stairs, they race toward the kitchen to get outside.

It only takes a few minutes for them to do what they need to and come back inside. By the time they are ready to come back inside, I have a pot of coffee brewing for Ryker when he wakes up. I turn back toward the cabinets to grab a few mugs and a wall of warmth envelopes me from behind. I melt back into him for a moment as he glides his hands down my curves.

"Darlin', seeing your ass peak out from under my shirt is one hell of a way to start my day." His gravelly morning voice does things to me that make me hate the fact we can't have a little fun this morning.

"How about I make you dinner in just one of your shirts?" I lift my arms, looping them around his neck as I arch my back and grind my ass into him.

"Fuck me," he groans against me as his nails bite into the flesh of my hips. "I'm going to die waiting until tonight." He admits which only makes me giggle, his dick noticeably hardens against my ass when I do.

"Oh my, you were serious about the giggling." I spin around and press my lips against his for a moment. My breasts flush against his chest, I can feel my nipples pebble against him with my own arousal. Rykers hands drop to my ass, and he lifts me onto the counter. The coffee long forgotten. Before he can deepen the connection of our kiss or go any farther, a throat clears behind us. He stiffens and turns his head to see Jake.

"Out, give me a minute," He snaps at his friend.

"Damn all you need is a minute? Fallon, if you need any help, let me know." Jake teases as he ducks back out of the house onto the patio.

I can't hold back the laughter as Ry drops his head to my shoulder.

"I'm going to kill him," he groans.

"No, you won't, but I'll go back upstairs so you two can have your coffee. I can use another couple of hours of shut eye," I admit, still laughing. Ry helps me down onto my feet and smacks my ass as I rush out of the room, the dogs close behind.

Thankful it's Saturday, I climb the stairs and go back to bed with the dogs. I collapse on my side of the bed with Haley and Marlow sandwiching me in. Everything over the past twenty-four hours is racing and replaying through my mind on repeat. My cheeks hurt from how big my smile is. I don't know that I've ever been so happy. My eyes close as I start to doze, not ready enough to face the day.

An annoying ding sounds from my phone with a notification, my eyes flutter open taking in my surroundings. I stretch and yawn before I lift myself up onto my elbows to see the phone is laying on the nightstand on the charger. I grin, knowing that he must have grabbed it before he found me downstairs this morning because it was still in the bathroom when everything happened last night.

Once I unlock the phone, I notice it's already after eleven a.m. and see a text from Elle which makes me blush so fiercely, I cover my face with my hands for a moment before I can find it in me to respond.

After our text exchange and she tells me she's on her way I climb out of bed and rush back into the bathroom to wash up before she gets here. I rush through the motions of washing myself off, once I turn off the shower and grab a towel, I slide open the shower curtain to find Marlow and Haley laying on the floor next to the shower.

"Go on you two, I'm not leaving you." I laugh, feeling a little guilty they were locked out all last night. I'll have to make it a point to let them back in after from now on. The towel easily wraps around my body which I still find incredibly satisfying. Being a heavier girl my entire life, finding towels large enough to tie around me has always been a challenge.

Several moments later I'm dressed in a long green floral print sundress and sandals. Since Elle wanted to hang out here, I may have forgotten the panties. What Ry doesn't know won't kill him...for now.

Chapter Twenty-Eight

Jake has been giving me shit all morning, starting from the moment I let him back into the house for coffee and he hasn't let up. The shit-head is so amused at me finally sealing the deal, his words, not mine, that he's been trying to get the details. I get it, Fallon is gorgeous. However, I also know that he and Elle have been tiptoeing around each other for months. They need to just get together already.

"Ryker! Man, what's the plan now?" He asks as we approach the house.

"What do you mean?" I turn toward him in confusion.

"You don't do long term, not since Lex," the look on his face tells me he thinks I'm insane.

"Until now," I level him with a look.

"For real?"

Ignoring his question, I continue on until I reach the patio where I see Fallon and Elle seated at one of the tables. My face splits into a grin when I see my girl. She's dressed in a long green sundress that somehow accentuates her curves while not being clingy.

"Hey, beautiful," I put a pep in my step to get to her faster.

"Aw, hey bestie! I've missed you too," Elle greets me.

"Eh, you're alright," I bend at the waist to press my lips to Fallon's. "But you don't hold a candle to my girl, here." Fallon blushes, her hands cupping my cheeks as she dives in for a deeper kiss. "Fuck, I missed you."

"You're both gross. It's been like what, five minutes?" Elle teases.

"What are you doing here?" Jake chimes in from beside me. He's got his arms crossed over his chest, shooting a glare at Elle.

"Uh, visiting my friends, what's it to you?" Annoyance is clear in her voice. Jake huffs in response as he starts to walk away.

"Do you want your food or not, dick?" She asks, Jake stops and turns back toward the three of us.

Fallon and I exchange a look; she's just as confused and amused by the confrontation happening before us as I am.

"You brought me food?" Jake cocks a brow in disbelief.

"Of course I did, I'm not a monster." She sighs and pushes a container of Chinese food toward the opposite end of the table.

I shrug and take a seat next to my woman. Her dress starts to ride ridiculously high up her thigh as she moves around in her seat. Her creamy, bare thigh is on display, and I can't help but rest my hand on her skin. She shivers at the connection, obviously affected by my touch. I lean over into her space and press a chaste kiss to her the sensitive spot on her collarbone.

We continue chatting for a while before Elle and Jake decide it's time to leave and it takes everything in me not to cheer. Elle and Fallon share a quick hug while Jake walks to his car, waving. I breathe a sigh of relief when they're finally gone. Reaching for Fallon, I pull her into me, my mouth crashing against hers in a toe curling kiss. When my hands trail down her body to cup her ass, I find she's bare. *Fuck me.*

"Darlin', I'm not waiting until dinner," I toss her over my shoulder, a loud laugh bursting free at the sudden movement. I carry her across the patio and into the house. Once we're in the kitchen I sit her on the counter. "I'm going to fuck you on this counter like I wanted to when I found you down here this morning." My voice sounds different, laced with a primal need I've only fantasized about.

She whimpers at my words, the feeling obviously mutual. With a wicked grin, I lift the skirt of her dress up to her hips, exposing her bare pussy. Leaning down, I spread her legs apart just before swiping my tongue up her slit. She moans at the sudden sensation. I chuckle darkly and stand to kiss her one more time.

"I want you to play with your pretty little pussy while I get the condoms. Do not make yourself come, understood?" The command is deep, leaving no room for argument.

"Y –ye – yes!" She stutters out her response.

I rush out of the kitchen, racing up the stairs to grab the condoms from the bedroom. My cock is pulsing as the fabric of my jeans tightens, strangling my length with how hard this woman has me. Once the strip of condoms is in hand, I race back down to the kitchen. The sound of her moans travel through the hall, and it only makes me more eager to be inside her again.

When I reach the kitchen, I find Fallon with her fingers circling her clit, her head leaning back against the cabinet door with her eyes closed and mouth slack as she rides out the pleasure. God damn, she's stunning. I cross the space in two swift steps, startling her. Her eyes fly open when she feels my hands on her thighs.

"Fuck me, Ry," she pleads.

Wasting no time, I unhook my jeans and shove them down my hips far enough to free my cock. I lift a foil packet to my lips and tear it open with my teeth. A light sheen of sweat coats Fallon's skin as I slide the condom on. She's on the verge of coming and I'm not sure I'm going to last much longer. I step forward, notching myself at her entrance and grip her hips, my nails biting into the plump flesh of her round ass. We both groan as I slide inside her.

"Fuck, Darlin'," I groan as soon as I'm fully seated. I drag her ass closer to the edge as I thrust inside her, pumping my hips slowly.

She throws her head back and cries out when I swipe my thumb over her clit, methodically circling as I continue fucking her at a leisurely pace. I don't want this to be over too soon. Sweat threatens to drip down my face as she cries out again.

"Please! I need – Oh god!" She begs for her release.

I pick up my speed and fuck her with abandon. Fallon's arms loop around my neck as I lean down and bite a nipple through the fabric of her dress. She screams at the dueling sensations of pleasure and pain.. Tingles race down my spine to my balls. The thrusts of my hips become erratic as I approach the edge. I pinch her clit between my fingers, her pussy convulsing around my cock and any self-control I had disappears.

"Fuck! Fallon!" I groan

"Ry! Yes!" She moans my name so loudly it spurs on my release.

Jesus Christ

Mrs. Addams, Elle, and I have been working together all morning to get dishes prepared for the fourth of July party she's hosting at Ryker's. He's so close to his parents, his mom in particular. It's so heartwarming, and such a difference from what I'm used to with my own family. Large bowls filled to the brim with an array of salads; fruit, potato, ambrosia and Caesar with homemade dressing take up every shelf in the two outdoor refrigerators hidden in a storage shed. Elle is chopping vegetables for a veggie tray, while I'm in the midst of making a huge pan of mac and cheese.

"Fallon, sweetheart," Mrs. Addams calls for my attention. I look over my shoulder to see an older man that could pass for Ryker's older brother. My lips form a shy smile as I take the man in. He looks so much like his son; the only difference is his hair has more gray throughout and his face has noticeable lines from years lived. "I'd like to introduce you to my husband, Herbert."

"Hi!" I stop mixing and drop the spoon onto the counter. Quickly turning around, I wipe my hands on the apron I'm wearing. "It's so great to finally meet you!"

"Hi, Fallon," He grins in response. "I've heard so much about you."

We spend a few minutes chatting before he excuses himself to help Ryker get the food on the grill before guests start to arrive. Mrs. Addams follows her husband out while Elle and I finish up.

"Can we change upstairs before –," her words are cut off when Jake walks in with both arms full of bags of chips.

"Coming through!" He announces as he drops them on the table.

"Hell no, Jake! You can grab the bowls for the chips, you know where Momma Addams keeps them. Make yourself useful!" Elle chastises him.

A look passes between the two, and I cover my mouth to try to hide the smile.

"We'll be down in a bit. Finish up for us please, Jake? Thanks!" My hand finds hers and I drag her out of the kitchen. When we reach the stairs, I stop and turn back to her. "What was that about?"

Elle glances behind her toward the kitchen and gestures for me to go all the way up to the bedroom. She starts to pace as I take a seat on the bed watching with curiosity. It takes several minutes of her spiraling before she speaks.

"We slept together," she whisper yells at me.

"You and Jake?" I whisper yell back, my eyebrows nearly in my hairline.

"No, you and me." She rolls her eyes, heaving out an exasperated breath. "Yes of course, Jake and me!" She's a little louder this time and pushes me in the shoulder like she can't believe I would make her say it out loud.

My mind whirls with amusement as I attempt to find the right words for her current state. She hasn't stopped moving, so I place my hands on her shoulders, holding her still. She stares at me with unshed tears in her eyes.

"When? And why is this a bad thing?" I ask her, concerned by her reaction.

"Two months ago; it was a drunken night of loneliness, and he's acted weird toward me ever since." She admits, her voice wobbling with emotion.

My eyes go wide at the realization. "It was just before Ry and I met, wasn't it?" Tears fall down her cheeks as she nods. I wrap her in a tight embrace and hold her while she lets out her stress over the last couple of months.

"Why didn't you tell me?" I ask.

"You've been so happy with Ryker; I didn't want to bring you down." She cries into my shoulder.

"Babe, we're supposed to be here for one another," I squeeze a little tighter for a moment before continuing. "I can compartmentalize my relationship with Ry and hate Jake with you."

"You're a good friend, he really sucks." The sobs seem to wain while we sit and talk.

"I love you too," I hold her for a few more moments reminding her just how much of a badass she is before she stands up and declares it's time to look hot so she can show him what he's missing.

Forty-five minutes later we're walking down to the patio with our hair and makeup done. She chose a short, flowy white floral sundress for me to wear. The green and white floral pattern makes my naturally tan skin look like it's glowing. Meanwhile, I talked her into her denim mini dress that shows off her toned legs. Her breasts are lifted to the gods with the built-in bra and her light brown hair is styled in a loose braid laying over her shoulder. No man at the party will be able to keep their eyes off her. Well, no man except mine.

As soon as we get into the kitchen, I grab us both a Twisted Tea from the fridge before we head out to join the others. I loop my arm through hers and lead her outside. The moment we emerge from the house, the chattering and conversations abruptly stop. With a quick glance, I realize everyone truly does have their eyes on Elle. She's as red as a ripe Jersey tomato. A grin twists my lips as soon as I see Ryker walking towards us.

"Hey, Darlin'," he presses a kiss to my forehead. "Elle, it's very weird to say this to you, but you look gorgeous." He scrunches up his face in faux disgust. "I don't like it." His teasing tone brings a smile to her face and the embarrassment seems to fade.

"I hate you," Elle states very matter of fact before she disappears into the crowd around us.

Looking around, I realize the patio and backyard are filled with bodies. I've never seen so many people at one party. Honestly, I didn't even know there were this many people in town.

"Fallon," Ryker says my name, amused like it's not the first time he's tried to get my attention. "You are a vision in white."

Now it's my turn to blush.

Chapter Thirty

The moment Fallon comes into view my heart gets caught in my throat. She's gorgeous. Momma and Dad told me today just how much they like her and it's the first time my dad has made it out here since they got back from their trip. I know the look on my face must resemble that of a kid on Christmas. Then Elle walks out of my house behind Fallon and she's a knockout, which is completely weird and I'm not sure how I feel about her finding her inner woman. She's like a little sister, it's just odd to see. I glance over my shoulder at Jake, my friend obviously affected if the way he's gawking at her is anything to go by. I chuckle before crossing over to the girls.

After a few minutes with them, I pull Fallon along with me to introduce her to everyone. I know she's been here for about six months now, but this is the first Addams' family barbecue she's attended. At least half of the people here spend most of their time on their land. We spend a good while going from person to person until she's finally met everyone.

After I'm confident she's put in enough of an appearance to ease her own mind I pull her aside. Once we reach a cluster of chairs no one is hovering around I drag her down onto my lap for a few moments alone. For the first time today, I can sense her body relax as I wrap her in an embrace.

"Darlin', this dress is doing things to me." I admit as I stare into her blue eyes that constantly take my breath away. A wicked grin plays at my lips, "tell me you're wearing panties underneath or I'm sending everyone home right now."

She smacks my chest with a giggle that sends blood straight to my cock. God damn.

"Ry, do you think I would go commando when I know your parents are here?" She smirks.

"To torment me? Yes, yes you would." Her eyes are alight with mischief at my words.

"Ok, yes I would, but not with everyone else here!" She's got a wicked grin on her face and it makes her beautiful features even more striking.

My mouth finds hers and we share a chaste kiss before I let her pull away. She smiles shyly at me before standing to rejoin everyone.

I cross the patio to where Jake is seated next to the fire pit we haven't lit yet. It's too warm this afternoon for that. His forlorn expression is quite pitiful. With a dramatic sigh I sit down next to him and stare at him, waiting for an explanation.

"What?" He doesn't bother making eye contact.

My chest rumbles with laughter.

"Since when are you a comedian?" I ask, "What's the problem? Why are you over here pouting, this isn't you."

"Nothing, I don't want to talk about it." He attempts to wave me off.

"Bullshit—talk." I admonish the kid. He's Elle's age, not much of a kid anymore but still he's younger than me. I've known him for about half as long, but we've been friends for years now. I know when he's being a dumbass.

"You're going to be pissed at me." He groans as he leans forward, and his head drops into his hands.

"It's possible I'm going to be pissed at you no matter what because you're not acting like the normal shithead I know and tolerate," I grumble teasingly.

"About two months ago," he begins and takes a swig of his beer. "I was out and saw Elle. We were both drinking. Things may have gotten… physical." I notice a flinch as he glances at me.

"Ok, you're adults. Get to the point of the story," I urge him to continue. Jake may have dated more than me, but he's never stuck around with anyone for more than a few months. If he's only been with Elle once and is still hung up on her to the extent it's affecting his mood all this time later, there is more of a spark than he wants to admit.

"Well, it was right before you met Fallon and took over her deliveries. She thought I was avoiding her because I hadn't come back by." An annoyed huff sounds before he says, "I like her, but she refused to listen to me when I tried to tell her what happened. She's been putting me through hell since."

"So," I tilt my beer toward where the girl in question stands. "Go claim her in front of everyone." My shoulders lift in a casual shrug like it should be obvious.

Jake's lips twitch for half a second like he's considering it, but shakes his head violently, like it's the worst idea he's ever heard.

"Have you met her? If I go up to her and try to stake my claim in front of everyone without her wanting me, she'll knee me in the balls." He cringes, shifting slightly in his seat.

With a roll of my eyes, I nod in the direction Fallon and Elle are standing talking to a few of the guys from Bailey's farm.

"When was the last time you've seen her dressed like *that* for a damn barbecue?" The amused snort leaves my lips before I can stop it.

He laughs and nods his head before his eyes go wide and I turn in the direction he's looking. I half expect to see Elle and one of the Bailey's getting handsy. But I'm left speechless when my gaze lands on what has his eyes bugging out of his head. Memories of my past invade my thoughts.

We're huddled up at my locker, she has tears streaming down her cheeks as I hold her tight. Her dad was offered a job last night on the opposite side of the country. They have to leave within the week for him to start when they want him to. My blood boils as the pain of losing her radiates through my entire being. She's my first love, we were supposed to end up like my parents. High school sweethearts with the happily ever after.

"What if you stay with my family?" I ask as I cup her head into my chest, "I'm sure Momma and Dad would be happy to have you."

"I asked my parents already if I could stay with Courtney." She explains through sobs, "they say that we're family and we aren't going to be separated."

My heart hurts, I don't want to let her go. I can't lose her, not like this.

"We'll figure it out, maybe we can visit each other, yea?" I ask, my voice more hopeful than anything.

Does she even want to make this work or is this all me?

"I'll be in a different time zone, Ryker. How can it work?" She chokes out, "They think I'm too young to commit and I have no choice but to do what they say."

She pulls away and presses a kiss to my cheek. We stare at each other for a few moments, not saying anything. We just take one another in before she lets out a strangled cry and runs off down the hall.

It was the last time I would see her.

I shake my head free of a time so long ago.

"Is that? It can't be." Jake whispers from beside me as we stand.

"Lexi," I rasp in surprise.

Chapter Thirty-One

My eyes flicker over to where the guys are talking. I'm going to have to give him a heads up on what's going on with Elle and Jake. I'm not sure how he'll react, considering how close he is to both of them, but when she stops coming around Jake, he'll have questions. I can't help but smile when my gaze lands on him. The man has my mouth watering every time I see him. How I got so lucky to be his, I'll never know.

I'm about to excuse myself so I can join him for a bit when I notice his muscles stiffen under his black T-shirt. I look in the direction he's staring to see a beautiful, slim woman walk toward them. Her honey blonde hair is incredibly long and pin straight, it reminds me of how they used to style on Jersey Shore back in the day. She's stunning, with high cheekbones and a button nose that are to die for.

My body tenses as I watch the scene unfold. Ryker and Jake stand and greet the woman. Jake turns in my direction and I can see a pensive expression on his face which has me immediately concerned. The woman leans in and presses a kiss to his cheek which he doesn't try to deny. I turn back to the conversation with Elle and the Bailey brothers who she has been shamelessly flirting with the last few minutes.

"Excuse us, I just need to talk to Elle for a second, I'll give her right back." I smile as sweetly as I can.

I loop my arm around hers to pull her away to somewhere a bit more private.

"What's up, Bestie Boo?" She asks, but her face falls when she sees my expression.

"Who is he talking to?" My voice shakes as I ask the question.

I squeeze my eyes closed, as tightly as I can. Whatever is set to come from her mouth is going to break my heart. I just know it.

"No. Why the fuck is Lexi here?" She snarls. Her eyes are wide, and her face heats to a bright red as her body radiates with anger. Obviously, there is no love lost there.

My eyes are filled with tears as I open them and take in the expression on my friend's face, my chest heaving as the reality of what's happening sinks in. Lexi's hand is caressing his forearm. Was any of this real? It was a joke after all, wasn't it?

"I think I need to go." I whisper to her and quietly rush back inside before she can stop me. Marlow and Haley are following close behind and I've never been so thankful that they're my shadows.

We rush up to Ryker's room and I stand there for a moment, allowing the pain to wash over me. As I glance around and see the memories of the past few months and what he's done for me, my heart aches. I thought it was real. I thought we were – I shake the thought out of my head. I can't do this, not when it so clearly didn't mean the same thing to him.

The bag I need to grab is in the closet, so I march forward and pull it from its place. Once I have it out, I struggle briefly as I lift it on top of the bed to fill with everything I've brought over here. It should be like I never existed in his space. Who knows how soon he'll have her staying here. Will she warm my spot in his bed before I even land in mine?

Fresh tears fall as I close my suitcase and carry it down the steps. The dogs follow close behind, not leaving my side as I head out to the front of the house where my car is parked. I quietly load the heavy bag and slide in. Thankfully, I didn't finish my drink from earlier, so I turn over the engine and leave the place I was starting to call home. Any buzz I had vanished the moment she stepped up to him and he didn't walk away. I refuse to ask anyone for help, or to bring attention to my stupidity.

My drive so far is smooth, it helps that I refuse to go over the speed limit. Considering how hard I've been crying, I'm shocked I haven't been pulled over for swerving or some shit.

Everything about today had been perfect. His parents welcomed me into their lives. His friends and neighbors, people I had met previously and strangers I had thoroughly enjoyed getting to know had let me in too. All of it was a waste. He never wanted to keep me long term. It was just until she came back. The way they were so familiar with one another just proves it; she was his endgame. I was just a bump in the road to pass some time.

Sobs wrack through my body as soon as my car is parked. My stomach turns as I open the door and slide out. After I catch my breath, I unload everything from my car and carry it upstairs. Haley and Marlow are on my heels again, they won't let me out of their sight, their doggy senses telling them something is wrong. I slide the key into the deadbolt, unlocking the door. Once we're inside and the door is closed, there's no holding back the tears. Barely a few steps into my sanctuary, I stumble backward. I feel my back slam against a wall where I slide down, unable to hold myself up any longer. My legs pull into my chest, and I wrap my arms around my shins as I lay my head on my knees. It's not the most comfortable position, but it's better than nothing.

Unsure how much time has passed; my eyes flutter open. My gaze darts to the window where the sky is dark. I hear soft snoring from the couch, when my line-of-sight lands there, I notice Elle is sound asleep. My heart aches to know she cares enough to stay with me. She must think I'm insane. I should have stuck to my gut feeling and never have let this happen. I'm going to lose her just like I've lost him.

Marlow and Haley startle when I stand, my joints stiff from falling asleep against a wall with my legs curled into my chest for half the night. A strangled groan escapes as I take the first few steps to my room. Once we're there, I climb into bed, both dogs jumping on with me. I bury my face under the blankets in a sad attempt to block out the world.

We're not in here for long before my bed dips. I startle and throw the covers off to see Elle sitting next to me with a sad smile. My heart aches more at the closeness even if I need the person who has become my best friend. I scoot myself over, disrupting Haley but she moves with only a small argument and lays back down. Elle and I lay like that for a while, no words exchanging between the two of us. Just her presence is enough to calm my anxieties enough to try to sleep. At least, for now.

Chapter Thirty-Two

The years have been good to Lexi; she's still as beautiful as ever, even if they took her away from me. After the past few months, though, I finally understand why. Fallon was meant to be mine. I'm not entirely sure how long Lexi and I chat; it seems as though we're able to pick up right where we left off all those years ago, except something's different. Those feelings of first loves and broken dreams are no longer there. Not since someone else has taken up the space in my heart.

Laughter echoes around us as Lexi and I catch up on our lives since she left. An overwhelming shock comes over me when she tells me she's never been married. That was her entire life plan when we were kids. She wanted to get married as soon as we graduated, which I was fine with at the time. The plan back then had always been to find what Momma and

Dad have. Happily ever after with my high school sweetheart had been the dream, until Fallon. As the time passes while we catch up, I'm glad things didn't work out that way. As beautiful as she is, Lexi isn't the girl for me.

"I always pictured you with the white picket fence and two-story ranch with two point five kids by now." A deep chuckle escapes in response to the latest revelation.

"You took over the farm, yea? Where is your wife and kids?" She's got a flirtatious smile on her face.

"I just started seeing my girlfriend a couple of months ago." I feel my face flush, I may have been thinking about it, but I know she's not ready yet. "We'll get there."

She glances around as if she's trying to find someone.

"Well, where is this mystery woman?" Her smile turns calculated, I can't quite put my finger on what she's getting at, but it sets me slightly on edge.

When I look around, I notice everyone has left, only a few stragglers remain in clusters chatting away. The sun is long gone beneath the horizon and I can't help but wonder why Fallon didn't come get me to go to bed.

"She's probably in bed. She's been waking up with me in the morning lately." I smile at the thought of Fallon waiting for me in my bed.

"Well, if she's already asleep, how about I stay over and keep you company tonight?" The wicked grin on her pouty pink lips is one that used to tempt me. Right now I'm just in shock at her brazen request.

"It was good catching up with you Lex, take care of yourself. If you're going to be here for a while, I'll introduce you to Fallon." As much as I try to hide the disgust in my voice, I know it's still there. I leave her sitting alone, irritated at her offer.

I walk into the house after saying goodnight to those who are still here. There tend to be a handful of people that crash in the yard, pitching tents when the nights are warm like this. As soon as I walk inside, I notice the dog's bowls are missing. *Huh, weird.* I climb the stairs to my room expecting to hear Marlow and Haley jumping around as soon as they sense my approach.

Nothing happens. No paws padding on the floor, no dog nails clicking around with excitement. What the hell is going on? When I reach my bedroom to find it empty, my heart sinks. What the fuck is going on? And more importantly, where the hell is Fallon?

I run to the bathroom to find it empty as well, her toiletries and hair tools are gone. None of her clothes are here. All the dog's toys are gone. She's gone. I pull my phone from my pocket and tap furiously until I see her contact. I press the picture of her beautiful face with the most incredible smile you'll ever see. The line doesn't even ring, it goes straight to voicemail. What the fuck? Tapping again until I find Elle, this time it rings but she doesn't answer. My heart is beating like a snare drum in my chest.

My feet move before my mind has a chance to catch up. I'm out the front door, snatching the keys off the hook as I march outside. The truck is right where I left it, and I leap off the porch, dashing for the driver side door. Gravel flies from my tires as I floor it and head toward Fallon's. The dark road is illuminated only by the passing street lamps as I fly down the road. With no fucks given about traffic laws, I arrive in record time. Fallon's car isn't here and there's no lights on at her place or Elle's, but at least Elle's car is here.

I throw the truck in park, not even bothering to close the door as I run to the front. The main door is unlocked, so I step inside and knock on

Elle's door. Nothing. I hear nothing and there is no movement inside. What the fuck? I try to call both girls again with no luck.

After another twenty minutes or so of knocking on the door, I climb back into my truck and get back onto the road. My heart hurts as I drive blindly through town. I don't know where to go, just that I can't give up looking for her. Where the fuck would she go? What the fuck is going on?

The sun is starting to rise as I pull back up to my house. What is usually my favorite time of the day, being able to see the exact moment night changes to morning, has now become something I dread. The breathtaking colors as the sky brightens into new possibilities seems tainted by not knowing where Fallon is. There are a few cars scattered around the yard from those who stayed over. My mind whirls with confusion and my chest aches with pain as I climb the steps to the porch. I startle when I walk into the kitchen to find Jake. We usually take the day after a party off. He's drinking coffee in my house. On a day he doesn't need to be.

"What are you doing here?" My tone is clipped when I ask the question.

"Checking on my friend. Were you completely trashed or just a fucking idiot?" He arches a brow as he takes a sip of his coffee and hands me a mug.

"What the hell are you talking about?" I drink the bitter liquid; a new pain shoots through my heart when I think of her not making me try her flavored coffees.

"You ditched Fallon," he cocks a brow. "For Lexi, of all people in the world?" Jake's eyes are filled with a rage I don't understand. Why the hell does he care this much?

"What are you talking about? We just talked!" Thoughts of last night fill my mind. I was catching up with a friend. Nothing happened that would make Fallon run like this. None of it makes sense. I wrack my brain, sifting through all of our past conversations, confusion clouding my mind. And then it hits me. *Oh god.*

Chapter Thirty-Three

Rays of sun shine through my bedroom curtains. Haley and Marlow are still snoring on either side of me, their body heat combined with the blankets making my body feel too warm. Memories of last night assault me. Even knowing what Kyle had done, he still didn't have the decency to end things with me before running back to his ex. At least it wasn't with Elle, strangely I find comfort in that I still have my best friend. Even if she's friends with him.

Tears stream down my cheeks again as I bury my face into Haley's furry red neck. My arms wrap tightly around her as I hold her close. She answers by scooting back into me, her way of comforting me. Marlow lays on the other side with his head resting heavily on my hip. I know they're worried. I hate feeling like this. I hate that my brain tells me that

I'm not good enough, that I should have known this is how it would end.

A soft knock startles me from my cocoon of warmth and dog cuddles,and I cautiously roll over to see Elle standing in the doorway to my bedroom. She smiles warmly at me and crosses the room to sit next to me on the bed with a cup of coffee from The Caffeinated Pumpkin. A wave of emotion overwhelms me as I fling myself onto her. Fresh tears begin to fall as she carefully places the to-go cup on the bed side table.

"Thank you for being with me." I cry into her shoulder.

"Bestie Boo, I'm pissed at him too. But there is a lot of history there that you don't know about." She sighs as she releases me.

"What do you mean?" I ask as I slide up to lean against the headboard.

"Lexi wasn't all sunshine and rainbows like he remembers. He and I rarely hung out back when they were together. And it wasn't because of the age difference, even if it's just a couple of years. He would always include me in anything he did up until they started dating. I stopped coming around if I knew she was at the farm." She explains, her eyes are set off in the distance as she goes down memory lane. "Lexi would make it a point to make it known that my friendship with Ryker was one sided, to the point of bringing me to tears. She would tell me over and over again that Ryker didn't like me, that he just dealt with me because his parents told him to. She even went so far to spread lies about me trying to get him to sleep with me." Elle wipes away a lone tear as she recounts her history with this evil woman.

"Why didn't he stop it?" I ask, angry for a young Elle.

"He never knew about the last part. Me not coming around, he thought it was because I was growing up and wanted to do my own thing." She shrugs, resigned to the memory.

Fury rages through my veins as I think of what she put Elle through. I hate Lexi.

A low knock startles me awake. He's knocking on my door again. Marlow and Haley jump on the bed, ready to dart from the room.

"Stay. It's ok. Quiet." I tell them, amazed that they listen. Especially Haley, since she usually has opinions she likes to share. The number of times she's howled, growled, and groaned at me when something is going on that she feels needs to be discussed is quite comical.

I hear him storm down the stairs again when I don't answer. It's been two days, and if I'm honest, I'm shocked he even cares enough to come by. For a moment I wonder if I left something there that he's trying to return. I flop back onto the bed and groan; the dogs settle in as we fall back asleep.

Elle and I are having dinner together tonight, a little earlier than I normally like to eat. It's the first time I've been out of bed and showered since I left his house a few days ago. Even if she's forcing me to be a human right now, I don't feel like one. We're in front of my TV watching some romantic comedy. Well, it's supposed to be a comedy. Tears silently fall from my eyes again; I place my plate on the coffee table before I bring my knees into my chest.

"Fallon?" My friend's concern is palpable.

"Why am I not good enough?" I stare at her through the tears. A need for someone to put into words what's wrong with me is so strong it nearly knocks me off my feet. "In high school, I was only ever good enough for one friend. Kids used to make fun of me for my weight, 'Watch out or she'll hit you with an udder,' was shouted so many times as I walked through the halls. I've had more one night stands than I've had relationships." I admit through sobs. "My high school boyfriend only dated me because he went to a different school, then he broke up with me for someone thinner. Then there was Kyle who we all know is a piece of shit in his own right. Now, Ry? For his high school girlfriend?"

My breath hitches as I think about my past. About everything that I've been through. "The only family I had is gone. My biological father was a fuckwit who left before I was even a year old and haven't heard from him since. You'd think when he found out my mom was in a car accident and died when I was ten, he would have tried to be there, right?" A strangled laugh erupts from my throat as I continue. "He wasn't even there for the funeral. I lived with my grandparents until I was eighteen."

Elle wraps an arm around my shoulders, pulling me to her side. I rest my head on her shoulder, my body shuddering with silent sobs. "Sweetie, there isn't anything wrong with you. Your first boyfriend was young. Fuck him. Kyle and Ruth were both the worst kind of trash and honestly, they did you a favor. From what you said, the dick was mediocre at best." She shudders at the memories of those conversations when I had first moved here, and she got me drunk, so I'd drop my walls. "Ryker? Until I can see straight enough to have a conversation with him, I won't be able to give you insight there. Jake says that he's broken up about you disappearing though."

With tears still streaming down my face I glance back up at her.

"You've been talking to Jake?" My heart may be shredded but I know my friend has feelings for him.

"Yea, we don't need to talk about it though." She says, trying to brush off the only bit of happy news I've had in days.

"No. Distract me with your happiness," I practically beg her.

The brightest smile splits her face as she recounts asking Jake to hide my car so Ryker wouldn't know I was home and how it led to them growing closer over the last few days. She's so incredibly happy which makes me feel better, even if just a little bit.

Chapter Thirty-Four

A searing pain shoots through my hand as the skin tears apart. The sensation of blood trickling down my knuckles only pisses me off even more. When I pull my hand from the hole, I've punched into the side of one of the tool sheds, I see just how badly I screwed myself. I'm halfway to the door when I hear the sound of gravel crunching under tires as someone pulls up my drive. *Fan – fucking – tastic.*

"Ryker Jordan Addams! Get your behind out here right now!" Momma hollers from next to her car.

I turn toward her with my hand up in front of my face. When she sees me, her eyes widen in horror. Momma rushes over to me and leads me inside like a child by my ear. An annoyed groan leaves me as I follow her. Once we're inside, she pulls me into the kitchen where I sit at the table.

She rushes around grabbing a towel and water to clean the wound. But before she starts, she smacks me upside my head.

"What the hell, Momma!" I growl and rub the sting with my good hand.

"I don't care how old you are, child; I will take you over my knee if need be," She quips. "What the hell is wrong with you?"

"What isn't?" I grumble as she takes her time methodically cleaning the cuts around my knuckles. Once the blood has been wiped away and the antiseptic has been applied, she bandages me up just like she used to when I would get into shit that I shouldn't.

"Talk to me Ryker. What the hell are you doing?" She stares at me as she takes a seat in the chair across from me.

"I messed up, Momma. Fallon saw me talking to Lexi and I— I just didn't think," I explain, "we were just catching up. A couple of friends. I didn't think anything of it." I drag my good hand through my growing beard. I haven't shaved since she left me. "I've been trying to find her, to explain."

Never one to shy away from my emotions, tears freely drip from my eyes as my mom watches me closely. She arches a brow as she considers what to say next. I drop my head into my hand as the silence grows unbearable.

"I didn't even know about Fallon; I was here about Elle." She chuckles, "But now that I know all these details..." She stands up and thwacks me on the side of my head again. "What in the actual – excuse my French – heck is wrong with you?"

"Wait, is Elle, ok? She hasn't spoken to me either!" I stand from my seat and step to pace when Momma's small hand wraps around my wrist and pulls me back to my ass.

"Do you remember when you started dating Lexi?" The question is rhetorical, "Elle stopped coming by. The poor girl would run off quicker than Dorothy threatening Ma with Shady Pines if you were home."

"Yea, she was just growing up and didn't want the person who she saw as a big brother hovering." I cock a brow at her, "why?"

"Ryker Jordan Addams, I swear I raised you to be smarter than this." She shakes her head at me, "She avoided you like Uncle Don avoided paying taxes because Lexi was a little bitch to her."

My eyes go wide as my mind wraps around her using such a vulgar term, at least for her.

"What are you talking about? Lexi and Elle were never together." I ask, memories of our past filter through my mind, and I try to remember a time when Lexi and Elle were in the same room. "What did she do?"

"A whole laundry list of things. She made that poor girl go home crying more than once. Spread rumors about her relationship with you." Momma shakes her head.

"How do you even know all of this?" I can't grasp why Lexi would have done this. Elle has always been a little sister to me. What was the point?

"Honey, she's always been like a daughter to me as much as she's been a little sister to you. She shared a lot with me." She shakes her head. "Now go get off your ass and make this right with both of them. If I hear you're being friendly with Lexi again, boy, I will take you over my knee. I don't care how old you are, you're still my child."

My truck approaches The Caffeinated Pumpkin, and I can see Elle through the window as I park. She's cleaning the counter and chatting with a customer. I hop out of the truck and move quickly across the lot to enter before she can stop me like she has every damn time I've been by here since this all went to shit. As soon as I get to the door, she's there with the lock turned, keeping me from entering.

She holds up the same sign as every other day I've tried to come talk to her that says *Deliveries will only be accepted from Jake – Ryker Jordan Addams is not welcome in this establishment until further notice. x Elle Belle.* The nickname I used to call her when we were kids rips through me. I want to scream through the glass. *I didn't know!* It pisses me off that I didn't realize what was happening at the time. I keep my eyes on Elle in hopes that she can see my sincerity, but she ignores whatever she sees and waves me away.

I storm away from the door. I know I'm acting like a petulant child but damn it, I'm trying and neither of them will let me explain anything. Frustration flows through me and I walk back to my truck. As soon as I shift into drive, I'm headed in the direction of the shelter. It's thankfully only a minute drive to get there. When I pull into a parking spot, I shut off the engine and hop out, my destination clear in my mind.

When I enter, Fallon's office is empty. Not of stuff, all her personal items are still taking up space but she's not here. It doesn't look like she's been here since I visited last week. I walk out to the adoption office and stop one of the volunteers.

"Excuse me, I'm looking for Fallon. She's not in her office." I look at the young man expectantly.

"Uh, she's working from home this week. She's sick or something." He stares at me for several moments before responding. The answer comes quickly once he starts speaking. As if it's practiced.

"She's. Sick." I repeat the words one at a time. "Thank you."

My feet take me to my truck without me really thinking about it. She's not home. I've been to her place multiple times. Her car isn't there, plus there's no way the dogs wouldn't bark if they heard me coming.

Once I'm back in the truck, I start the engine and drive around aimlessly again. This time my next stop is the motel on the other end of town. It's the only place I haven't checked. For the life of me, I can't imagine she would stay there even to get away from me, but until I can see her again, I have to do something to try to find her.

U nable to take any more time off, I told everyone at the shelter I was going to be working remotely. If anyone asks, I'm sick. It's not exactly a lie, not exactly the truth either though, I suppose. My heart hurts as I start an email from the shelter account to Mrs. Addams.

From: Hollow Heights Animal Shelter

To: Colleen Addams

Subject: Pumpkin Fest Adoption Event

Hello Mrs. Addams,

Fallon asked that I reach out to you to get the ball rolling on the up-coming event that was agreed upon at the Addams' Pumpkin Farm. She has handed this to me to plan as she has too much on her plate at the moment with the shelter being at capacity. I was hoping we could

run through some ideas that she had mentioned when she delegated
the task to me.
Thank you
Hollow Heights Animal Shelter Team

The painful ache in my chest only grows as I type the email. Lies make me sick to my stomach, but I know there is no way I'd be able to handle having a conversation with her. She seemed so sincere about my relationship, or lack thereof, with her son. The idea of her being as heartbroken as I am makes it worse. At the same time, the idea of her being happy about us no longer being together makes the idea of her knowing it's me makes me want to crawl back in bed for the rest of my life.

A response comes more quickly than I anticipated.

From: Colleen Addams
To: Hollow Heights Animal Shelter
Subject: RE: Pumpkin Fest Adoption Event
Of course, please let Fallon know I'm thinking of her. What ideas did you have? As you know, we usually have hay bale wagon rides for the younger children. And then we have traditional wagon rides into the patches for anyone to pick pumpkins. Elle brings out coffee and treats for everyone.
Mrs. Colleen Addams

I send my response with the hope that we can make this work.

To: Colleen Addams
Subject: RE: RE: Pumpkin Fest Adoption Event
Mrs. Addams,

> *The usual is fantastic, we were hoping to do a photobooth setup with a pumpkin throne for the dogs to sit on. Do you think that's possible? We can request a few food trucks to come out as well. There are a few that have adopted from us and love to show their support any way they can. Thank you.*
>
> *Hollow Heights Animal Shelter Team*

My day is split between contacting rescues for placements, reaching out to current and previous fosters, as well as posting across all of our social media platforms.

Seemingly on the same page after only a few messages, my heart feels fuller. Mrs. Addams seemed to be fishing at one point with her response. But when I ignored the question she had asked about if the staff member I was pretending to be would ask the real me if I would like to meet her and Ryker for lunch she went back to the topic at hand. For the first time since this all happened, I'm smiling. This event is still going to happen. I just may not be here when it does.

Chapter Thirty-Six

The past two weeks have been nausea inducing if I'm honest. Most of my time was spent in bed doing the bare minimum to keep my job. Taking the dogs out into the back yard was the most exercise I've had, and I hate it. So, today is my first day back at the shelter. When I decided yesterday to rejoin the land of the living, I sent an email to make it clear to anyone present that the only people allowed in my office are staff and volunteers.

Ryker hasn't stopped trying to reach out to me. Elle said he's tried to talk to her at The Caffeinated Pumpkin, but she keeps locking him out. Jake has come by every night for the past week to have dinner with Elle and me, but he's made it a point to not talk about him.

The drive to work this morning is quick and easy. When I arrive, I pull my car around the back of the building and park out of view. Dramatic?

Maybe. But Ryker has been determined, and I just can't handle seeing him yet. Marlow and Haley are excited to get out and be around people so much that they race to the back door and wait for me to let them in. Once the door is open, they're off and looking for all of their favorite people. For the first time in two weeks, I smile a genuine smile. I just hope where I end up will allow me to bring them in with me.

My computer starts pinging with notifications the moment I turn it on. We've had such an incredible response from vendors looking to make the Pumpkin Fest at the Addams Farm even bigger. It will bring in more money for Ryker and the community at large with how many people are showing interest, plus the fact that animals will be adopted! My next few hours are spent replying to messages, calling vendors and getting the information over to Mrs. Addams for confirmation she feels they're all a good fit for the festival. Once that's done, my daily calls to rescues are made to see if we can get any of the animals to a safe home or facility. We're getting close to capacity again. It's a never-ending revolving door of animals being found on the streets or being surrendered by their owners for one reason or another.

My stomach growls and I groan when I look at my phone to see it's already noon. I step out into the hall to see Shelby walking toward me with a large bag. I arch a brow at her in question.

"I don't know what the hell is going on with you two, but that man would *not* stop calling me unless I promised to pick up lunch for you." She rolls her eyes.

"He what?" I glance down at the bag and back to Shelby.

"Yea babe, my husband was ready to go up to the farm and lay him on his ass." She chuckles. "It's so sexy when they get possessive like that, isn't it?"

I can't help but snort at her comment, I wouldn't know. She hands me the bag which I cautiously take. What's his deal? I groan to myself as I turn back and sit at my desk to eat.

Elle strolls out to my car from her shop. Her smiling face brightens my day, and I can't help but flash my own smile back at her. She opens the passenger door and slides in, buckling her seatbelt before we're off toward the market.

"What happened today that's got you so smiley?" I ask.

She shrugs her shoulders like she doesn't want to respond.

"Spill it, sister."

"Ok fine! Jake came by and spent the afternoon with me while I got stuff ready for tomorrow. It was just nice being around him." She's practically glowing.

"I'm so happy for you," I grin. I really am happy for her. My pain will not dilute my joy for her happiness.

"Enough about me, what do you want to do for dinner this week? I'm thinking some of your barbeque chicken and I can make roasted potatoes."

"Sure, sounds good." I reply as I pull into the parking lot.

As soon as we're out of the car, Elle takes my hand and leads me into the market. We've got what we need but are still perusing the shelves to see if anything else jumps out at us. She's searching for a particular brand of pickles she's been hearing about when I see Lexi approaching. My heart starts pounding in my chest, the rhythm picking up as she gets closer. Why is she still here?

"Hey, Elle Belle!" She calls, Elle stands quickly and goes stiff next to me.

"What do you want, Lexi?" She asks.

"What, I can't say 'hi' to an old friend?" Lexi giggles.

"If we were friends, sure, but we weren't. So, again. What do you want?" I've never seen Elle so angry. Lexi ignores my bestie, instead turning her attention my way.

"Hi! I'm so sorry, I didn't see you there. I'm Lexi, and you are?"

"Fallon," my name is the only thing I can verbalize at this moment.

"Ahh!" She cries out like she's just discovered the secrets of Atlantis. "You're friends with my boyfriend, Ryker. Right?"

My vision blurs at her words. I fucking knew it.

"I'm so glad I was able to run into you actually!" She grins wickedly.

"Why?" I ask, trying in vain to hide the tremble in my voice.

"I just wanted to thank you for keeping my side of the bed warm." A sardonic giggle passes her lips. "Now that I'm back, he can actually enjoy where he's sticking his dick. Not having to use the new fat girl to pass time."

My heart plummets to the floor at her words.

"Let me tell you, he's been very attentive since you've been gone." The sinister grin on her face is my last straw. I'm tired of girls like this.

My hand balls into a fist and I swing. I don't know how many times I land on her before Elle has me back in the car. When I look down at my hands I notice blood dripping from my knuckles. It's not all mine, which makes me happier than it should. Violence isn't usually the answer, but right now? Right now, that little bitch deserved every last mark I gave her.

"Jesus, Bestie Boo! Are you ok?" Elle cries out as she gets me in the passenger seat of my car.

"Oh god, I've never hit someone before," I admit, flexing my already swelling knuckles.

"She deserved it," Elle giggles as she drives us back to our place.

Chapter Thirty-Seven

The lack of sleep is getting even worse. I've been of minimal help to Jake, who's essentially running the whole damn farm while I've been wallowing in my self pity. Already on my second cup of coffee this morning and it's only two a.m. Sadly it isn't doing much of anything for me. I stand in my kitchen at the sink just to glare out the window. It's still dark so I walk outside and sit on the porch swing. Stars are the only thing that light up the country sky. It's usually so peaceful. But not tonight. Not any night since Fallon's been gone.

"Fe – he – he – he – heeeeneeyyyy!" I call out half-heartedly. A flash of red darts across the porch and then he's in my lap. A smile pulls at my lips as I pet the fox. He's been sticking around closer than usual since Fallon left. It's obvious he can tell just how depressed this entire fucking situation has made me. We sit like that for a few hours, with me mindlessly petting him as his little chirps and snores are the only sound filling the early morning air.

I barely register that the sun has begun to rise in the horizon when I hear the crunch of gravel under heavy tires. The sound is the only warning I get that Jake is here and ready to start his day. He hasn't bothered to talk to me about what my plan is for the day's tasks anymore. He just gets it all done, taking up the slack without any argument. I need to give him a raise. Jake jumps from his car and storms over to where Mr. Feeny and I are sitting. As soon as he is on the porch the fox dashes out of sight and back into hiding.

"Are you with Lexi again?" The accusation is the first thing out of his mouth as he gets close to my face. His cheeks are red with anger, eyes blazing in fury. He's ready to fight and I'm on my feet in an instant, even though I don't understand what's going on.

"What the hell are you talking about?" My brow furrows with confusion at his words. "Why the hell would you think I'm with Lex?"

"Ryker, you're my best friend, but don't be a dumbass." He snarls at me. His jaw flexes for a moment before he walks away.

I'm frozen in place as thoughts rush through my mind. Guilt, sadness, anger. My brain decides to go with the latter. Fury floods my veins; I rush inside and grab my keys. The past two weeks have been a cluster fuck of a nightmare. When I walk back outside to my truck, Jake's truck is still where he parked but he's no longer in sight. I climb into the driver's seat and start driving toward town. After a few hours of driving around and a fresh tank of gas later I find myself sitting outside of the shelter. I can't do this anymore. I need to see her.

I climb out of the truck and walk toward the entrance of the Hollow Heights Animal Shelter. As I approach Fallon's office, I feel a hand on my forearm. The person I find attached to the hand is the same young man I had seen the last time I was here. He has a shy smile on his face. Obviously uncomfortable about something.

"Sir, only staff and volunteers are allowed back here." He says as he nods back toward the office.

"Excuse me," I growl and attempt to walk past him. The kid side steps to mirror my position and block me. He didn't seem comfortable telling me the rule, but when it came time to enforce it, he showed up. Well, I can't fault him for protecting her. I am thankful for that at least. Annoyed, I turn back toward the door, fed up with all of this.

Somehow, I'm going to get her to talk to me so we can figure this out. I feel defeated yet determined when I walk back outside. As soon as I'm by my truck, I hear a familiar voice. I inwardly groan as Lexi approaches me. She is the reason all of this started. I don't turn toward her voice in hopes that I can just leave, but she's at my side before I can get away.

"Hey, Babe!" She smiles so brightly. "How are you?"

"I really don't have time right now, Lexi," my response is short, but she doesn't take the hint as she paws at my arm. I turn to face her, my irritated expression turns to shock when I see her face. She's swollen and her face is covered in angry purple bruises. "What the hell happened to you?"

"You can't make time for me even though 'what's her name' punched me?" Her giggle used to be infectious, now it only makes me cringe. "I wanted to see if you would like to go to dinner with me this weekend. Maybe we can see if things pick up where they left off." She leans her body into me, and I stiffen before stepping away.

"No, I told you, I'm with Fallon." Now my growl is toward her and the fucking audacity.

"You mean the fat girl?" She asks, sounding chipper and proud.

"Excuse me? Say that again," I dare her.

"You know, the fat girl that hangs out with your precious Elle Belle." She smirks before continuing. "I told her that we were together when I saw her last night, so it's fine. She knows. I mean everyone says that she isn't returning your calls anyway, so I was just helping show her that you moved on."

My jaw flexes as I take in what she's said. Anger isn't a strong enough word to describe just how upset I am. I ball my hands into fists at my sides before I speak again.

"If you ever speak about her or anyone in that manner again, any time you spend in this town will be a living nightmare. Do you understand me? She is mine just as much as I am hers, you vapid bitch."

"Ryker!" She screams as I climb into my truck and drive away.

Fallon

A heavy sigh drawls free as I hover over the button. Once I do this it will be my tenth completed application. This one could be incredible. It's in Chicago, I would be able to move into a city and become invisible again. Just go to work, do my thing, and come home. There's an ache in my chest as I click submit.

Just then Jake strolls into my apartment. Elle hasn't outwardly told me, but they've been all but inseparable since I left Ryker's. Since he and Elle have been together, Jake's made himself right at home. If she's not downstairs, he walks his happy ass straight up the steps and lets himself in. They're kind of adorable.

Elle jumps to her feet and runs over to him. She's wrapped around him like a koala before he has a chance to react. Luckily, he has already put the pizza we ordered on the table. Jake's arms cinch around her, keeping her tight as they share a passionate kiss. It's kind of hot but also gross. *Get a room.* Ok, I may be a little jealous. We don't need to talk about it. I chuckle to myself as I stand and walk into the kitchen while they get their greeting out of the way. Once the plates are out of the cabinet, I put a couple of slices on each before I head out to the living room and sit back on the couch.

"Can you at least tell me that y'all are together for real and not just messing around?" I tease.

"We are," Jake announces with a wide grin. "Together I mean. Right?" He glances at Elle with confusion.

"Yes, babe," she giggles, "we're together."

They cuddle into each other and kiss again for a brief moment. When they separate this time Jake's attention is on me.

"Fal," Jake calls my name, or well, an abbreviation of my name. I'm not sure how I like it yet.

"Jake," I say all serious, unable to hide the giggle after a few seconds.

"I need to tell you something," his cautious tone has me on edge.

"If it's about him dating Lexi, I already know. We saw her at the market yesterday evening and I punched her in the face." I shrug like it's no big deal.

"Bestie Boo! You didn't just punch her, you wailed on her! I would have been worried about her if I didn't hate her so much." Elle snorts.

Jake freezes as his gaze bounces from Elle back to me and back to her again.

"You – you what?" He stutters.

"It's why we asked you to pick up pizza. We had planned on cooking." Elle giggles as she wraps herself around the man even tighter than before.

He looks back and forth between the two of us again like he's seeing us in a whole new light. Several moments pass before he finds his voice, when he speaks, he says, "What did she say to set you off like that? I may not know you that well, but I know you're not going to go Amanda Nunes on someone without reason."

My brow furrows, the name sounds so familiar. After a moment of reflection, I realize what he's talking about. I throw a napkin at him as I chuckle at the reference to Ronda Rousey's last UFC match.

"She told us that they're back together and that he's enjoying himself in bed now that he's with her." I let out a dejected sigh. "It's not anything I didn't already suspect, but how she said it was too much."

My mind runs through the confrontation again. She was claiming her territory, she made it clear that I was never more than a way to pass time for Ryker.

"She was being a cunt." Elle announces as she grabs her own plate and joins me on the couch.

"Fal, I don't think they're together. When I called him out this morning, he didn't know what I was talking about." Jake glances at Elle who shrugs before he continues, "she hasn't been at the house either. He's not even working with me. The first couple days he wouldn't even acknowledge me. He seems down, I don't think he's slept."

"Jake, stop. I've applied to ten shelters out of the area and out of the state." Leveling him with a gaze before I continue, "I can't have hope when I know what I saw and what she told us. Elle was right next to me when she said what she did."

I stand at the doorway stunned in silence when I find Kyle with Ruth. I gasp loudly at the shock. She glances over her shoulder and her eyes meet

mine. Instead of a look of guilt I glance into a pair of hazel eyes that have a look of pride as she screams for Kyle to fuck her harder. I nearly vomit as he digs his nails into her hips and fucks her in our bed so hard that the headboard bangs against the wall.

The memory fades and quickly transforms into my nightmare.

Ryker and Lexi are lying in bed together, the afterglow of sex on their skin. They're cuddled together in the bed that we shared. She giggles as she tells him about how she claimed him in front of Elle and me. In a flash she's on top of him, riding his cock. Her head falls back between her shoulders, her long hair a curtain over her small round ass as she calls out his name.

I startle awake with sobs reverberating through my body. Tears flood my eyes as they fall freely. Anger follows closely behind. Why my sub-conscious feels the need to torture me like this, I don't know. But it's fucking infuriating. Flashes of the look in his eyes as he was with her in my nightmare hurt worse than when I found Kyle and Ruth in my actual bed. Marlow and Haley are curled in a cuddle puddle behind me. Haley lifts her head and flops it down in the crook of my neck. At least I know they're not leaving me.

Chapter Thirty-Nine

Sleep has evaded me for I'm not even sure how many days. I'm sitting on the stoop outside of The Caffeinated Pumpkin. The sun is rising beautifully in the distance as I glance down at my watch, the display showing six a.m., when I hear footsteps approaching. A soft startled gasp sounds, I take a deep breath, and I look up into the eyes of my best friend.

"Hey, Elle." I whisper, exhaustion clear in my voice.

She doesn't speak for what feels like ages, her eyes locked on me as I sit in front of her. I know I'm forcing her hand to speak, but I can't keep going the way I've been. I know that.

"What are you doing here, Ryker?" She sneers and crosses her arms over her chest as she waits for my response.

"I didn't know. I swear to you I didn't know." My gaze is locked on her as tears fall. "You are my best friend. The little sister I never knew I wanted. If I had known, I would never have stayed with her as long as I did."

"That's great, but you're back with her now," Elle growls as she steps aside to let herself in.

I'm on my feet in an instant following her into the shop.

"I'm not. I'm in love with Fallon." I argue, my voice hoarse.

"Then why were you so comfortable and touchy with her? We saw you." Elle's voice is full of accusations, which I know I deserve.

"Fallon is the only person I want. I was shocked to see Lexi, that's all. I realize I should have handled it differently, but there was nothing romantic about the one, well two conversations we've had." I rush out in one breath.

My feet have a mind of their own as I pace back and forth in front of the counter as Elle starts her opening checklist. I can feel her eyes boring into me and I let out a low growl.

"She stopped me outside of the shelter when I tried to see Fallon and told me what she said to you both. I've never wanted to hit a woman as badly as I did then." I admit.

Elle's chortle startles me. "Don't worry, Fallon took care of that for you."

"I know, Lexi tried to make it seem like Fallon was behind it before showing her true colors." My blood boils as the memory repeats in my mind.

Elle cocks a brow at me. Her thoughts are written so clearly across her face. She's warring with herself to give me any information.

"It took two of us to pull Fallon off Lexi and I had to drag her out." She speaks as though she's in awe of the memory.

"Thank you for looking out for her when I couldn't." My heart is still aching over the loss, I can't handle this. I need to get Fallon back.

"She's my best friend," Elle shrugs as if it's a no brainer.

"Elle, I love her. I love her more than I've ever loved anyone." I admit. "I appreciate that you've been taking care of her, but please. I need to see her. I need to make this right." I'm begging, I don't even care. All that matters is getting Fallon back.

Elle stops in her tracks; her eyes glued to me. I can see the wheels turning in her mind as she contemplates her next move. My eyes are filled with tears as I wait for her decision.

"Please, Elle." I whisper as a tear falls free.

Her face softens for a moment as she takes me in. She towers over me when she approaches. It takes a moment for me to realize I've fallen to my knees. Elle's arm wraps around my shoulders before she speaks.

"You should go apply to volunteer at the shelter. Get as many hours in as you can before she leaves." Elle's words shock me. "Fallon's been applying for positions in bigger cities. She wants to run from the pain and the memories." She pauses for a moment, pity in her eyes, "from you." The realization from the words spoken has my stomach twisted in painful knots.

"Fallon's leaving?" I choke out.

"She hasn't been offered a position anywhere yet, but she's been actively applying for a few days." Elle's voice is filled with sadness as she speaks.

"I have to go." I rush out of The Caffeinated Pumpkin and jump into my truck.

A short drive later, I park in front of the familiar building, racing inside. I stop at the front desk to fill out a volunteer application. The same young man that I've seen twice before is behind the desk. He cocks a brow at me when he notices I'm filling out a volunteer application.

"I'm Alex," the kid extends his hand to shake.

I accept the gesture, grasping his hand in mine. A throaty chuckle erupts from my throat when he tries to squeeze my hand harder to establish dominance. Nice try kid. If he thinks he has a shot with my girl, he's sorely mistaken. I'll fucking burn down the whole damn town before I let her go.

"Why do you want to volunteer here?" The question is an accusation. He's a smart kid.

"To get back the love of my life." I say honestly, like there could possibly be any other reason.

After the paperwork is completed, he takes me through a quick run-down of what is expected of me. What I'm allowed and not allowed to do as a volunteer. Alex walks me through the kennels, indicating colored stickers as to which dogs require more training to be able to interact with. It's something that Fallon started when she first got here.

Our training lasts another hour before he tells me I'm free to interact with the animals as much as I like, but just the animals. He glares at me. Trying to hide my smirk, I nod and head out to the kennels. When I'm sure he's gone, I grin to myself before sneaking back inside and heading toward Fallon's office.

My heart beats wildly in my chest as I get closer. Her door is closed when I approach, a light sheen of sweat coating my skin once I stop in front of the thin piece of wood. Memories I've shared with the woman behind this door flood my mind. My heart fills with emotions knowing I'm about to see her. With a deep breath, I tap softly and wait for her response.

Tears prick at my eyes when I hear her voice.

"Come in," she calls out cheerfully.

Chapter Forty

"**H**ey, Darlin'," his voice breaks through the sound of the clicking of my keyboard as I type a response to his mother of all people.

"What are you doing here, Ry?" I swallow hard as I raise my gaze to meet his.

He still looks as sexy as ever. A dark T-shirt stretched taut over his broad chest; a pair of dark wash Wranglers cover his lower half. When I meet his gaze the organ in my chest stutters. Dark circles under his eyes show his exhaustion is as prominent as mine.

"I needed to see you. To talk to you." He steps toward me, and I glance down at my hands.

He inches closer and I curse myself for leaving Marlow and Haley at home today.

"There's nothing for us to talk about, Ry," I whisper. "Please. Just go."

Tears I thought had stopped are pricking at my eyes yet again. He's standing in front of me when I look back up. Ryker raises his hands; he goes to brush the tears from my cheeks, but I flinch and pull away.

"Beautiful, please," he starts, "I swear to you, I'm not with her. I haven't been with her since high school. *You* are the one I want."

"Ry, just go." I'm trying to hold myself together as he speaks. "I can't do this, not here. Not now."

A throat clears from behind us.

"Ryker, get out of here." Tim's voice cuts through the tension in the room.

"No, we're talking this out." Ryker's response is blunt and harsh.

"Right now, you're done. Get out now or we'll revoke your volunteer status." Tim's venomous reply has me glancing up at him. His eyes are full of fire.

Ryker's eyes briefly leave my face to look at the man who is threatening him. They exchange a look that doesn't make any sense to me. "This isn't over Fallon. We *will* talk about this." With a long, low growl Ryker storms out of the office. "Thank you." I collapse in the desk chair as tears blur my vision.

"Fallon, why don't you head home. It's alright. We can cover everything for the rest of the day." Tim's voice is so soft as he places a gentle hand on my shoulder. "It's going to be ok."

My car comes to a stop in front of my place. He knows I'm still here, it's only a matter of time before he forces himself into this space. There's no point in hiding any longer.

Haley and Marlow greet me, bounding in to give me a hug as soon as I get in the door. I kneel before them, and they both perch their paws on my shoulders. Marlow's head on one shoulder, Haley's on the other. A loud sob bubbles up my throat as I wrap my arms around their furry bodies. I bury my face in Marlow's chest as the tears break through and flow freely. We sit there for a while before both dogs get down and run off to play. Once I gather my bearings I stand, slowly moving to my couch where I take a seat. I pull my knees into my chest as the day's events unravel in my mind. Who the hell let him volunteer?

His words from earlier replay vividly. *"Beautiful, please." He starts, "I swear to you, I'm not with her. I haven't been with her since high school. You are the one I want."*

How can he say that, not only when Elle and I saw their reunion but when she told us? She flat out told us that they were together. A groan leaves me as I bury my face in my knees, my hands wrapped protectively around my shins.

Sometime later, I haven't moved from my position, but I feel the couch dip. I lift my gaze just enough to make out Elle sitting next to me. She places a hand on my back as she rubs gentle circles around my shoulders.

"I take it that it didn't go well today?" She whispers, her voice has a guilty tinge as she speaks.

"What do you mean?" My head whips up and I glare at her. "You told him how to get into my office?"

She hangs her head for just a second before her eyes meet mine.

"He forced himself into the shop this morning and we talked," she admits. "For what it's worth. I don't think he's with her."

I don't bother responding. Anger radiates through my veins that will be misplaced if I try to speak now. I'm not ready to talk to him. I don't know if I ever will be. Elle continues her attempt to comfort me. Several minutes later I hear Jake's voice as he walks into my apartment.

"Hey ladies! I got Chinese!" A moment passes before he speaks again. "What happened?" He sounds ready to draw blood.

My lips twitch at his kindness.

"He came in today. Applied to be a volunteer and everything just to get back to my office. Apparently, your girlfriend gave him the idea." I grumble, shooting a glare at my best friend.

"Uh, Elle?" I hear him put something heavy on the kitchen counter.

"Fallon!" She thwacks my arm before she continues and goes into the conversation she had with Ryker.

As Elle goes into detail of what was said my heart aches. Could he have been telling the truth? It takes a few minutes for Elle to finish telling her story. A weird feeling possesses me as I rerun everything since the barbeque. Memories of the two of them sitting together are seared into my memory.

A loud knock startles me back to the present. I glance at Elle and Jake who stopped talking and look toward the door. With a loud groan I bury my face back into my knees.

"I'll get it." Jake's smooth voice breaks through calming my nerves. We all know who is on the other side of the door.

Jake's voice grows softer the further he walks from us as he approaches the door. I glance up just in time to see Jake grab hold of the knob and twist, the door swings open. He smiles widely as he greets the person on the other side. My eyes dart back down to my knees. I'm not ready to see him.

"Hey Ryker," Jake's voice is welcoming when he sees the man that has been haunting my every thought. Without warning a loud crunch and then a heavy thud sound from my front door. Elle and I look just in time to see Jake laying on the ground with his hands cupping his eye.

Chapter Forty-One

"Hey, Ryker," the moment Jake appears in Fallon's doorway, I see red. One of my best friends fucked the girl who is like a sister to me only to be answering my woman's door. Anger burns through me, like the heat of a brand leaving its mark on untouched flesh. He's on his ass with his hand cupping his cheek when Elle and Fallon come running over to us.

"What the fuck, Ryker? What is wrong with you?" Elle screams as she drops to her knees next to him. "Baby, are you ok?" She's got tears in her eyes.

"'Baby?' Shit I'm sorry, I thought..." There's no point in explaining what I thought.

He knows what I thought. Jake subtly jerks his head in Fallon's direction. I glance over to see Fallon with tears and anger in her eyes.

Haley and Marlow begin barking as they barrel through the apartment to see what the commotion is. As soon as their eyes find me; their whines fill the room. I kneel and greet them for a moment before I stand to find Fallon, but she's disappeared. Again.

Goddamnit.

I storm to the bedroom where I find her sitting on her bed with her knees pulled into her chest. Tears are pooling in her eyes. My boot taps the bedroom door a little harder than necessary to close it. The flimsy piece of wood slams closed. Fallon flinches as the loud noise.

"Darlin'," cautiously, I cross the room to stand in front of the bed.

"No," she whispers.

"Please, Darlin'," I beg. I just need her to let me explain.

"No, Ry," she sobs. "I can't live like this, there's no –"

"That's enough," I cut her off, my voice coming out harsher than I mean. She snaps her mouth shut at my tone.

My eyes bore into hers as I sit on the mattress next to her. Her breath catches when I turn my body toward her.

"Darlin', I understand that you're mad at me, and you have a right to be." I say as I take in her exhausted state. Her eyes are ringed with dark circles, much like the ones I'm sporting. Fallon's usual sass isn't there. She seems as broken as I feel. "I shouldn't have spoken to Lexi the way I had. There hasn't been anything romantic between us since before she left during high school." Fallon's eyes shine as tears fall, and with a deep breath I continue.

"That night I had no idea she was coming. I was shocked to see her. I should have handled it differently. I should have brought you over to introduce you the moment I saw her walking toward us. The second I realized you were gone, nothing mattered anymore. I don't know where you have been staying but this has been excruciating. I've spent every night driving around trying to figure out where you are so I could talk to you." My cheeks are covered in moisture as I continue. "Darlin', I've only seen Lexi one other time since the barbeque, and it was after she told you some lies about us. I swear to you, nothing has happened, and nothing will ever happen with her."

I search Fallon's eyes for something, anything, to tell me she's hearing me.

"Ry," she whispers. My heart aches at the use of the nickname. I don't know if she realizes she's used it multiple times today. "Why?"

"It's you, Fallon. It's been you since the first time you sassed me at The Caffeinated Pumpkin. I am so in love with you, there could never be anyone else."

A loud gasp rushes past her lips when I finish speaking. Instead of moving I sit still allowing her to get a good look at my sincerity. Fallon's eyes are on me, I can feel them burn through me. When several moments pass, she sniffles hard as she tries to find her voice.

"Ry, the last few weeks have been somehow worse than when I found Kyle and Ruth. Part of me knew that he and I wouldn't last." She says through sobs.

I extend my hand to hold hers, thankful when she doesn't push me away. As much as I want to, I don't dare try to push for more contact right now.

"Ruth seemed to be shady from the beginning, nothing ever seemed to be quite right. Kyle though, he tried too hard to make sure I knew that he could do better than me." A loud chortle sounds from her. "Losing the idea of the relationships I thought I had with them is what hurt the most." She admits.

"Darlin', I promise you –," she holds her hand up, effectively silencing me. My lips flatten into a hard line.

"As silly as it is, I thought we had a future." She breathes, nodding between us, "a real future."

"We do. Fallon, I swear to you. It's you, my present, my future. You are my life." I admit. As I crawl across the bed to kneel before her, I cup her cheeks, lifting her face, so she's forced to meet my gaze. "Darlin', it's you and me." I don't bother hiding the smirk that's on my lips now as I finish my thought, "And whatever animals you want to bring home."

A soft sweet smile forms on her face that melts my heart. I press my forehead against hers, the simple show of affection that I had to use for so long when we were interrupted any time I tried to kiss her. A heavy sigh passes my lips as I remember the last time we were interrupted.

"Ry." She half cries, half giggles as her hands lift to my wrists. Her chest heaves as a deep sigh breaks free, "I love you."

I pull back and stare into her eyes. Did she really just say that? Is this real life? Tears fill my own eyes as I take her in. Fuck, I love this woman with everything I am.

I dip my head and press my lips to hers. The kiss is slow and cautious at first, Fallon's hands are still wrapped tightly around my wrists, her nails bite into the skin. I don't let up, giving my all into this moment. The need to show her I'm in, all in with her has me inching closer. My tongue darts out with a swipe against her lips. She softly whimpers then stiffens. I smile to myself; she didn't want me to hear that. I nip at her bottom lip and grip her hair at the nape of her neck. She gasps, giving me the opening I need to deepen the kiss.

Chapter Forty-Two

Ryker's hands roaming over my body is like a balm to my soul, wandering across my skin like he can't get enough. A soft moan escapes my lips as he finds my breasts, his fingers toying with my already erect nipples through my thin shirt. Our mouths are fused together in the most passionate and exquisite kiss. We stay connected for a few minutes before he pulls away.

Large rough hands grip my ankles and pull them away from my body. I giggle when he manhandles me onto my back. His large frame settles between my thick thighs as he grinds his length against my core. My pussy convulses at the sensation and a whimper finds its way free.

"I've missed you so fucking much, Darlin'," Ry's gravelly voice sounds right next to my ear, the admission ends in a sexy frustrated groan.

"I've missed you." My fingers tangle into his hair as I pant my response.

A low growl rumbles free from Ryker's throat as he takes my wrists in one hand and pins them above my head. His lips find mine again for the briefest of moments before he trails kisses to my jaw and down my neck. His other hand is at the waistband of my leggings. I can feel his grin against my shoulder where he's been pressing kisses.

"Fallon, how attached to these pants are you?" The question is unexpected as he sits back on his heels and stares down at me.

"I don't know? They're just leggings –," I don't have a chance to finish my statement when he tears the seam. I gasp in shock.

His lips are back on the exposed skin at my shoulder from the tank top as he yanks the fabric down the thigh that is covered. My pussy is bare, having gone commando to avoid panty lines in the thin pants. Needy gasps bubble free from my throat, my hands find his hair again and he growls pinning me down again.

"Ry, please!" My breathy pants fill the room as I beg him for more.

"Beautiful, you will get everything you want as soon as I get my fill of you." He smirks before he slides down my body, several kisses landing on my soft stomach before his hands are pushing my legs apart, forcing me to bare myself to him. A long warm breath blows against my slit. He's tormenting me.

"Ry!" I beg again.

My breathing is erratic as he slides further down my body. Soft wet kisses trail down to the sensitive skin just above my clit. Ryker's eyes sparkle with excitement as he settles between my thighs. He inhales deeply taking in the scent of my arousal. My body quivers in anticipation when he dips his face and swipes his tongue up the length of my slit, lapping up the moisture he's caused before he swirls his tongue around the sensitive bundle of nerves.

"Oh god!" I cry out at the incredible sensation.

I feel his lips twitch between my legs in pride as he continues the elaborate assault of his tongue against my pussy. My legs wrap around his back holding him in place as he forces me to the edge with just his talented tongue. Ryker pulls back just before I can reach the peak which leaves me breathless and annoyed.

"Ry! Fuck, please!" I whine, "I was so close!"

"Beautiful, I'm not done with you yet." He smirks as he stands from the bed and peels his dark T-shirt off over his head, exposing each taut rippling muscle, inch by delicious inch. "Like what you see, Darlin'?" He calls me out as I watch him strip.

"God, yes." I admit, the wide grin spreading across my face.

He continues undressing, his eyes locked on mine. The moment his jeans are around his ankles my lips part. His beautiful thick cock pops free and stands at attention. I need to taste him. Quickly crawling across the bed, I reach for him and a dark chuckle passes his lips.

"Ry, please." My hand grips his cock as I draw him closer to me.

"Fuck, Fallon." The words are barely audible in the low growl. His lips press to mine for just a second before he pulls away. "I need to be inside you."

The words break through my need to taste him. There will be another time for that. My heart flutters as my gaze meets his and I nod. The most sinfully sexy smile twists his lips, and I melt back into the bed.

His body covers mine; his warmth sends goosebumps over my skin. A shy smile dances on my lips as he notches himself at my entrance. Ry's mouth crashes against mine as he slides in effortlessly. We both moan louder than either of us have been as he buries himself inside me. I'm reveling in the feel of him when I hear cheers.

"Yes! Get it Fallon!" Elle is whooping and clapping outside the door.

"Oh my god." My face burns with embarrassment.

"Get the hell out of here, we'll see you tomorrow." Ryker yells as he slowly pulls out and thrusts back inside me, the guttural moan that leaves me is louder than before. I hear Elle's giggle and Jake scolding her and urging her to leave.

The interruption does nothing to distract Ryker from what we both so obviously need. Breathy sobs escape me with every thrust inside me. My nails bite into the muscular flesh of his biceps as he continues fucking me. A long low growl sounds from his chest, his hand slides between us where we're connected. Using his fingers to methodically rub my clit sends me over the edge.

"Ryker! I'm coming!" I scream out so loud my voice cracks.

My pussy contracts around his length as his hips slap into mine one last time. He roars my name as he fills my cunt with his seed. He collapses on top of me, only holding himself up on his elbows so he doesn't crush me.

"I love you so fucking much, Fallon. You're it for me. I promise you. Forever." He buries his face in my neck as he slowly pulls out. His cum drips down my thighs which has my pussy feeling awfully needy already.

"I love you, Ry." I admit before I push him onto his back and climb on top of him. My mouth crashes against his again, only parting from him to say, "I need you."

His cock is hardening at my ass as my breasts taunt him hanging in front of his face. Ryker lifts up, taking my nipple in his mouth before his fingertips dig into my hips and he guides me back onto his cock, helping me sink down onto him.

Chapter Forty-Three

A few days later

The phone alarm blares and drags me out of unconsciousness, I quickly silence it before laying my head back on the pillow. Marlow grumbles as he lifts his head glaring at me and flops back down on the other side of Fallon. I roll onto my side to tuck myself against Fallon's back. She whines as she pulls the blanket back up over us. I chuckle as I press a kiss to the shell of her ear.

"Morning, Darlin'," I squeeze her tight before releasing her from my hold. "I'll be back up once Jake and I get done."

She grumbles something unintelligible and waves me away.

After quickly dressing I shove my phone into my back pocket. A quick check on the dogs and I can see they're still sound asleep, not ready to go out for the morning. I slowly walk down the steps as I rub the sleep from my eyes.

Jake is in the kitchen making coffee for the two of us. He hands me a full mug which I happily accept. His gaze is glued on my face when I look up at him after taking a long sip of the delicious bean juice.

"Listen, Jake –" I start but he cuts me off, holding a hand up to stop me from continuing.

"So, you were a dick and hit me because you thought I was sleeping with her." He goes on, "I can't blame you. I hadn't shared anything about Elle. Plus, her car was hidden in my garage."

"You had her car?" I cough, choking on my coffee as we stare at each other.

"Yup, what can I say, we were all pissed at you." He shrugs. "Can we get to work now?"

"No, hold on." I groan. "Did you tell Momma about what happened?" I ask the question; it's been bugging the hell out of me.

"Man, the entire town was here and saw you." He shakes his head, "It wasn't any of us, but I'm glad someone did." He lets out a wicked chuckle. Fucker.

"You're an ass." We exchange a knowing look and laugh together. "Thank you for making sure she was ok when she wouldn't let me." I extend my hand to his when he takes mine, I grip his tighter than necessary and his eyes go wide. "Don't fuck shit up with Elle or it will be more than a right hook."

"Jesus Christ, you two really are like siblings." Jake's annoyed groan fades as he takes his coffee out onto the porch.

A few hours later when I return to the house after our morning work is complete, I find the house empty again. My heart starts to race when I pull my phone from my pocket to see a message from Fallon. .

Fallon:

I couldn't sleep when you left so we're heading in early. I love you, see you soon.

A whoosh of air rushes from my lungs as I breathe again.

Ryker:

You scared the shit out of me when you weren't in bed when I came back in.

Fallon:

That's why I texted you, don't worry I'm only fifteen minutes down the road.

Ryker:

Coffee?

Fallon:

Is that even a question?

Ryker:

See you soon, Darlin'

My lips twitch as my heart returns to a normal rhythm. Here's to hoping she's ready to go along with my idea. I chuckle to myself as I walk to my truck.

I walk through the front entrance of Hollow Heights Animal Shelter with a fresh cup of coffee from Elle like I have so many times before. My feet carry me back toward her office when a heavy hand grips my forearm.

I glance up to see the young kid from my last few visits, Alex with a stern look on his face.

"Didn't we discuss that you are only allowed around the animals?" He cocks a brow at me.

"Kid, if you keep Fallon's coffee from her, you're asking for trouble." I chuckle.

"I'm not a kid." He snarls at me, and I can't help but laugh.

"Ok, Alex. Listen, if you want to go check with her that I'm allowed back there again I will wait here." I gesture for him to walk ahead of me.

He glares at me for a solid minute before disappearing down the hall and into Fallon's office. When he reappears a second later Fallon is by his side. His cheeks are flush with embarrassment as she walks with him toward me.

"Sorry," he grumbles as he walks past, and Fallon takes my hand leading me toward her office.

Quickly crossing the room, I place the cup of coffee on the desk before turning back to face her. I stalk toward her and cage her against the closed door. My lips crash against hers and my hands wrap around her hair as we deepen the kiss.

We're both panting once we separate, I adjust myself once her luscious body is no longer pressed against mine. Her tongue darts out as she licks her lips causing a low moan to leave me. She steps closer to me and takes my bulge in her hand.

"I want you to fuck my mouth." She whispers as she looks up at me through dark lashes.

"Fuck, Fallon." I groan and press a soft kiss against her already swollen lips. My forehead falls forward pressing gently against hers. "I wanted to discuss something with you. But if you keep talking like that, I'm going to carry you out to my truck and take you home before we get a chance to talk." I rasp.

"Discuss what?" She glances up at me, her eyes dart between mine as she tries to read me.

"Your address." I say with a sly smirk as I take her hand in mine and lead her over to her desk. Once she's in her chair I lean against the edge as she registers my words.

"I don't understand." She's adorably confused.

"Darlin', the past few weeks of you not being in my bed when I woke up have been the worst of my life. I know it's fast, but the idea of not having you in bed with me every night and morning is unbearable." Her hands are trembling in mine.

"You want me to move in with you?" She asks, her cheeks are tinged pink.

"More than anything," I assure the beautiful woman before me. Her large breasts bounce as she chokes out a gasp.

"Ok," Fallon's smile falters for a moment. "Wait, Marlow and Haley, the three of us are a package deal."

Laughter bursts from my lips at her reaction. I shake my head, an amused smile on my face.

"I would expect nothing less, beautiful."

Fallon

A couple of months later.

The pumpkin festival is underway. Everyone is all smiles as guests from Hallow Heights and the surrounding towns in Glasscock County filter into the parking area. It's so busy we've had to allow people to park along the drive.

With the room we have, Colleen wanted to have every available dog here for meet and greets. I grin to myself as I see Erin and Shelby taking over the introductions. Shelby has a couple meeting one of the available pups, a Golden Retriever Saint Bernard mix, Reba.

Colleen approaches as I watch everyone. My heart is full as I see people fill out paperwork to adopt the dogs they're finding. A soft cool hand cups my shoulder, and I smile.

"Hi, Colleen." I grin as I glance over to see her face. "Thank you so much for this. It's unbelievable"

"Sweetheart, anything you set your mind to is believable and achievable." Her voice is tender as she speaks.

"Thank you," I turn to her and hug her tightly. "You've been integral in making this a success."

Her cheeks flush at the compliment.

"Your ideas of adding in vendors and food trucks is what's made it so popular," she grins at me.

We stand there for several minutes before Elle and Jake walk up to us hand in hand. I feel Colleen's joy before she says a word. She claps her hands together and squeals just like she had when she saw Ryker and I together the first time. My giggle bursts free when I see Elle's cheeks go bright at the commotion.

"Forgive my French but it's about damn time!" Colleen cheers as Elle buries her face in Jake's chest. It's the first time she's seen them together since they've started dating, Elle has been nervous to go public after how they started.

"Pay up," Ryker says from behind me as he wraps his arms around my middle holding me close while Elle glares at him for the comment.

"I hate you." She groans as she digs into her pocket and hands over a twenty-dollar bill.

"If I didn't know any better, I would swear you were my child." Colleen chuckles as she pulls Elle in for a hug.

The four of us work the event the rest of the afternoon until the afternoon sun is high in the sky. As soon as I return to the adoption table, I find a group of volunteers with tears falling down their cheeks.

"What is it? What's wrong?" I ask as I rush up to them.

"They're all gone!" Shelby cheers. "Every single one has been adopted!"

"Shut your mouth!" I shout and clamp my hand over my mouth when I realize that I just yelled at my volunteers. Shelby doubles over in a fit of giggles as my expression changes as their words register in my mind. "They're all adopted?" I ask for clarification. Tears pricking at the corners of my own eyes.

"Yep! Every. Last. One." She enunciates each word clearly with the brightest smile.

"Oh my god!" I scream out into the open space around us.

Before anyone can say anything else, Ryker is in front of me, worry etched across his face. "What is it? What's wrong?"

"Nothing! They're all adopted!" I cheer with a giggle that has his eyes sparkling with excitement.

"Woman! Don't scare me like that!" He stands to his full height and playfully spanks my ass making me laugh again.

The last car is gone by four and the sun is just about set on the horizon. Ryker and I are standing on the back patio as Mr. Feeny pokes his head out from underneath the porch and prances over to us. We both chuckle when Haley and Marlow rush over to play with the fox. The three of them rush off into the yard and chase one another while we stand in place.

"I don't know what I expected but today was perfect and so far beyond any expectation I could have dreamed up." I breathe as my arms wrap tighter around Ryker's side.

I feel him stiffen and pull away. My heart races so fast in my chest I feel like I may faint. My eyes start to fill with tears again as he towers over me with his eyes on me.

"Darlin'," He grins his sinful grin at me. "There is something that may make it better."

Before I know how to react, he's down on one knee.

"Ry, what are you –" I try to ask, but he pulls my hands to his lips, kissing my knuckles to distract from my thoughts.

"Darlin'," he repeats. "From the moment I saw you at the coffee shop I knew there was something so special about you that you were going to turn my world upside down." His bright smile is infectious. "We may have had our ups and downs in the short time we've been together, but I don't want to go another day without making you mine in every way."

My eyes are brimming with tears as he pulls something from behind him.

It's the tiniest pumpkin I've ever seen. He lifts the top which is connected by a hinge and shows me a ring that has my jaw on the ground. A ring box made out of an actual pumpkin. He is perfect.

"Marry me, Darlin'. Let me tell the world you're mine." His voice sounds hoarse, when my eyes find his I can see the emotion written on his face.

"Yes, of course, yes!" I sob and drop to my knees in front of him. My hands shake as he places the vintage ring on my finger.

Once Ryker is back on his feet, he picks me up and twirls me in a circle. The three animals rush back toward us as soon as they see the commotion. The two dogs jump and bark at our feet as they sense the excitement. Ry dips his head to kiss me when Mr. Feeny climbs up his legs and curls around my neck, as he swats Ryker away.

"Oh, come on!" He groans.

I double over in a fit of giggles and Mr. Feeny lands on his feet in front of me, his sweet chirps fill the air almost like he's laughing at us as he runs away. Ry pulls me back up to stand in front of him.

"If either of you try anything, you're getting locked out in the hall tonight." He threatens Haley and Marlow as he drags me flush against his hard chest and presses his lips to mine. I giggle into the kiss as he swoops me into a dip which fills my stomach with butterflies. As soon as he has me back upright, I melt into him.

"I want to dance with you." I whisper the same words he said to me only a few months ago. "Forever."

Afterword

It's funny, when I came across the cover to this book I never thought I could write a small town romance. Then I see a group of pre-made covers posted by Nerd Sisters Designs – namely Hope, (I told you I will forever blame/thank you for this). I tried to fight my love for this cover but after a week and repeatedly seeing it pop up on my Facebook feed I couldn't deny the pull. I had been over 40k words into Pickle's story but the moment I gave in Fallon and Ryker's story came to me and wouldn't stop.

This is basically my love letter to animal rescue and pumpkin spice coffee. As a plus size girlie most of my life, animals have been the one constant who haven't judged or bullied me for my size, trauma, or my shy demeanor. Given the chance to include two of the fur-babies that helped me through so much in life I had to go all in. Hopefully allowing you to fall for Marlow and Haley too. If you've been around for a while you know that I have a history of mental health struggles, both of these fur babies in their own way saved me multiple time.

If you've stuck around this far, thank you. Your support means more to me than words in my vocabulary. And to those who have been in the position of starting over no matter what the reason you will find your people. You aren't alone in this world.

xx

LC

Acknowledgements

My family, your support during this journey has been incredible.

Tiesha – My PA. Lady, I don't know what I would do if you hadn't come into my life. Thank you for all of your hard work and helping me organize my chaos.

My alpha team, you are the MVP and I can't imagine this journey without you.

Sara - My boo. I'll forever be thankful that you slid into my DM's. You are phenomenal, and I love you!

K.D. - My ride or die, I love you and I'm so freaking proud of you!

QS – you ladies keep me sane and I love you.

To the FBI Agent who tracks my search history, this one probably wasn't that exciting for you.

Lastly, but most definitely not least, to every single one of you who has reached this page. There will never be enough words for me to express my love for you adequately. Thank you for reading this book book. I cannot wait to share additional stories with you!

I'm an introvert. Well, until you get to know me. Then I won't shut up. I'm married to my favorite PITA; he's the doctor to my Clara. (IYKYK). We have a little boy who is growing way too fast and is already way too smart for my own sanity. I've had an unhealthy obsession with *Gilmore Girls* and *Buffy the Vampire Slayer* for years. You'll see the references throughout my writing. I've loved reading for as long as I can remember, but physical books with traditional novel paper give me the ick! So, you'll find me reading on my Kindle or listening to audiobooks on the regular.

Be sure to stalk me on all of my socials here

More by L. Clara

Endgame

The Unexpected Series

The Unexpected Match

The Unexpected First

The Unexpected Reunion

The Unexpected Third

The Unexpected Dance (Coming late 2025)

Mafia Books

Ludovico's Vengeance

Dark Romance

Killer In Our Pocket

Smalltown

Pumpkin Spice and Mr. Right